BY FIRE, BY MOONLIGHT

Read all the Unicorns of Balinor books:

#1 The Road to Balinor
#2 Sunchaser's Quest
#3 Valley of Fear
#4 By Fire, By Moonlight

Coming soon . . .

#5 Search for the Star

UNICORNS OF BALINOR

BY FIRE, BY MOONLIGHT

MARY STANTON

AN
APPLE
PAPERBACK

SCHOLASTIC INC.
New York Toronto London Auckland Sydney
Mexico City New Delhi Hong Kong

Cover illustration by D. Craig

ISBN 0-439-06283-7

Text copyright © 1999 by Mary Stanton.
Cover illustration copyright © 1999 by Scholastic Inc.
All rights reserved. Published by Scholastic Inc.
SCHOLASTIC, APPLE PAPERBACKS, and associated logos are trademarks and/or registered trademarks of Scholastic Inc.

12 11 10 9 8 7 6 5 4 3   0 1 2 3 4/0

Printed in the U.S.A.   40
First Scholastic printing, September 1999

For
Anna Beth, Julie,
and
Erin Carter

BY FIRE, BY MOONLIGHT

1

A talanta, Dreamspeaker to the unicorns of the Celestial Valley herd, stood under the waterfall at the head of the Imperial River. The water ran over her flanks and hindquarters, dimming the silvery violet of her coat and plastering her silver mane against her graceful neck. Her crystal horn glittered in the sunlight.

She closed her eyes, grateful for the momentary peace in the Celestial Valley. There was trouble in Balinor, the world of humans that Atalanta and her kind had guarded for thousands of years. Last night, the Watching Pool had failed to deliver visions of the world below the Celestial Valley. This was the first time in the history of the Celestial Valley that the pool had failed her. This meant serious trouble. Trouble so dangerous that Atalanta had asked for help from the Deep Magic.

Last night, the Dreamspeaker had sent word

to the Old Mare of the Mountain. An ancient unicorn, perhaps even the very first unicorn, the Old Mare was the heart of the Deep Magic. If any being could help Princess Arianna and her Bonded unicorn, the Sunchaser, it was she.

And so Atalanta waited under the soothing waterfall.

"Atalanta!"

"Rednal?" She shook herself, sending diamondlike droplets flying. Rednal stood at the edge of the riverbank, worry in every line of his muscular body. All the unicorns in the Celestial Valley were bound by color to the rainbow spectrum; Rednal was a deep crimson, which signified his position as lead stallion of the red band. Rednal was even more than just that: He was a brother to the Sunchaser, the great bronze stallion who was Lord of the Animals in Balinor.

Atalanta arched her neck in greeting. "Has Tobiano returned, Rednal?" The sturdy black-and-white unicorn had been on a mission to help Arianna and the Sunchaser recover the Royal Scepter from the evil Shifter. He should have returned to the Celestial Valley long before this.

"No, Dreamspeaker."

Atalanta sighed gently. The Dreamspeaker had discovered that the evil Shifter had hidden the Royal Scepter in Castle Entia in the Valley of Fear. The Princess and the Sunchaser had recruited a loyal band of six to enter the Shifter's domain. Two foxes named Basil and Dill accompanied Arianna, the Sunchaser, Lori Carmichael, and Lincoln, the collie. Through the Watching Pool, Toby had reported that the band of six had landed on the shores of the Valley of Fear. Then the Watching Pool had gone dark. Tobiano himself had not returned. With the Watching Pool closed to Atalanta, Toby was her only source of information about the fate of the Princess and the Royal Scepter. "He will come in time," she said, more to reassure herself than anything else. "Has Numinor called for the rainbow, Rednal?"

"He has, Dreamspeaker. All are assembled beneath the Crystal Arch. The rainbow has been formed." Rednal switched his long crimson tail in pleasure. The rainbow was a beautiful sight, with all the Celestial Valley herd lined up according to their color bands. It made a fine display. But most important, the power of the herd together was far stronger than any one unicorn alone.

"Good. We will need their strength. I have called on the Old Mare of the Mountain, but she has not responded yet. With the help of the rainbow, I may get her here."

Rednal suppressed a snort of excitement. He stood aside as the beautiful Dreamspeaker waded out of the pool and onto the riverbank. He was sorry that the Dreamspeaker was distressed. Life in the Celestial Valley had been peaceful until a year ago, when the evil Shifter had begun a series of plots against the King and Queen of Balinor, their daughter, Arianna, and her brothers, the Princes. The Shifter had betrayed the Royal Family. He had stolen the Royal Scepter and had kidnapped the King, Queen, and Princes. Only the High Princess Arianna and the Sunchaser, the magnificent unicorn to whom she was Bonded, had escaped the Shifter's claws.

Rednal walked at her side. The two unicorns made their way up the riverbank and across the velvety meadow to the Crystal Arch. Atalanta was silent. A light breeze swept her silver mane across her face, hiding her violet eyes.

Finally, Rednal couldn't hold his questions back any longer. "Are Her Royal Highness and the Sunchaser in danger, Dreamspeaker? What have you seen in the Watching Pool? Will the Celestial Valley herd be called out to fight the Shifter?"

Atalanta didn't answer right away. They had reached a slight rise in the rolling valley. She stopped to gaze upon her home.

A green meadow rolled before them, starred with brilliantly colored flowers. The Crystal Arch rose high into the blue sky; the lower end led to Balinor, the upper to the reaches of the home of the One Who Rules. The Celestial Valley herd gathered in front of the Arch. The assembled unicorns were all the colors of the rainbow: from the red band of Rednal himself, through Larissa of the purple band.

"You will hear the answers to these questions in a moment, Rednal." With delicate steps, she trotted down the rise.

The Celestial unicorns quieted as Atalanta approached. Numinor, the Golden One, Lord of the Sun and lead stallion of the Celestial Valley herd, stood proudly in front of them. Atalanta took her place beside him. He bent his head and blew softly on her cheek in greeting.

Atalanta turned and faced her herdmates. Then, head high, she walked to the foot of the Crystal Arch. The base of the arch rose from a foundation of solid amethyst, the same magical rock that formed the Watching Pool half a league away. To the right of the stairs that led to the Crystal Arch was the gateway that led to Balinor below. The wall to the left was carved in intricate patterns of fruits and flowers and the paving in front of the wall was polished smooth. It looked like a glittering purple carpet flung down in the green grass of the surrounding meadow.

Atalanta positioned herself on the amethyst floor and bent her head so that her horn just grazed the surface. "They are lost," she whispered. "The Princess and the Sunchaser have disappeared from the Watching Pool. The last I saw of them, they had entered the Valley of Fear, where my magic will not take me. Worse yet, I cannot see in the Watching Pool at all! Some terrible evil has darkened the magic waters." A tear rolled down her cheek and splashed onto the jeweled rock.

Nothing stirred in the clear air. The sky was blue and quiet and the sun shone steadily. In the ranks of the rainbow, a unicorn sighed.

Atalanta spoke again, her sweet voice dark with sorrow. "Since Arianna and the Sunchaser crossed Demonview and went into the Valley of Fear, I have not heard from them. And last night, when I went to the Watching Pool, no visions came to me. We must know how to help the Princess and our brother Sunchaser. Do not tell me all is lost."

Another tear splashed onto the rock. It glittered in the sunlight, and an old, old voice said crossly:

"Stop splashing me!"

Atalanta stepped off the polished rock and onto the grass. As she and the other unicorns watched, the amethyst stone rolled, bulged, and grew into a large hump. Gradually, the rock smoothed out and took shape.

An ancient unicorn mare stood on the grass. Her horn was gnarled with age. Her coat was totally gray. Stiff white whiskers grew from her ears and muzzle. Only her eyes told of who she was and the power within her. They were as clear as water, as young as spring. And they seemed to see everything.

The Celestial Valley herd murmured among themselves, astonished. This was the Old Mare of the Mountain, bearer of the Deep Magic. Very few of the unicorns had ever seen her before, although all knew who she was. There must be true danger in Balinor if Atalanta had to call on her for help.

"Well!" said the Old Mare of the Mountain. "You'd better have a good reason for dragging me out of my nice sleep, Atalanta." She shook herself violently. Bits of hair from her coat floated in the air. She sneezed vigorously, then glanced at the Dreamspeaker with a critical eye. "You're not looking too fine, my girl. You seem to have lost Arianna, the Sunchaser, and her friends."

"Can you tell us where they are?" Atalanta's voice was soft but determined.

The Old Mare cocked her head to one side. "Thing is," she said, "they aren't supposed to be there. And they aren't supposed to have it with them."

"But *where* are they? And *what* aren't they supposed to have with them?" Atalanta asked. "The waters of the Watching Pool are dark! I cannot help them!"

"The balance of magic's been upset," the Old Mare said. "And you are going to have a time getting it right again." She rolled her bright eyes at Atalanta. She blew out as a horse does, with a sound like "paaah." As she blew, a silvery breath came from her mouth. It floated in the air, the thinnest of vapors. Then it began to move, to shape itself into a pair of scales. "The Scales of Magic," the Old Mare said. The scales were evenly balanced. "See? That's the

Shifter's side on the left. And your side, Dream-speaker, is on the right. They always go up and down a bit, but they're never really out of balance. But this is what Her Royal Highness did when she snatched the Royal Scepter out of Balinor."

The right side of the scales shot up. The left side went way down. A murmur of fear and aston-ishment swept the ranks of the rainbow herd. The balance of magic had never been upset before!

The Old Mare cocked her head. "Tsk, tsk, tsk. And now Her Royal Highness has to meet two chal-lenges to get the sides balanced again, because right now, the Shifter's got the advantage." She grew solemn. The Scales of Magic hung in the air, lop-sided and ominous. "There's going be a trial by fire." As she spoke the words, a weight shaped like a silver rose dropped onto the right bowl. The left side went up a bit. "And an ordeal by moonlight." A second sil-ver rose fell onto the right-hand bowl and the scales hung even. "That's if Her Royal Highness overcomes each trial. If not —" The two rose weights disap-peared. The right side shot up again into the air. Then the scales quivered, started to spin faster and faster, and disintegrated before the eyes of the horri-fied herd.

"Will Arianna win?" Atalanta asked, her voice somber.

The Old Mare shrugged. Slowly, the gray of her coat began to turn to rock again. The stone crept up her knees and past her withers.

8

"Please!" Atalanta cried, desperation in her voice. "Tell us what to do!"

"Humph!" The Old Mare yawned sleepily as the transformation from live flesh into stone crept past her neck. "Arianna, the Sunchaser, and Lori Carmichael jumped back through the Gap. Foolish. Only Lori was supposed to go, but I knew that this would happen. I tried to warn them, but *no*. Said so in the poem I gave them — 'three of Six shall not return.' But did they question which three? No. And they should have."

"They're on the other side of the Gap?" Atalanta took two steps nearer, perhaps in an attempt to stop the Old Mare's return to rock.

"And they've got the Scepter with them," the Old Mare said. "Bad business. Allows the Shifter to issue the two challenges to them, before they can come back to Balinor. And there's not a lot that you can do to . . ."

The Old Mare disappeared into stone. Atalanta pawed the grass, tearing up great patches of sod. She bowed her head in grief. "Oh, Princess. How can we help you now?"

2

A herd of shadow unicorns, eyes red with rage, black coats shiny with the sweat of fear, thundered down the sides of the mountain Demonview and into the Valley of Fear. Their iron horns were lowered; the deadly points were aimed at the hearts of any that rode against them. They raced across the Fiery Field, past the Pit where the slaves of the Shifter labored. Black clouds gathered and lightning forked the air.

A pair of foxes and a collie hid under a thorn tree and watched them pass. The collie, named Lincoln, was a tricolor of mahogany, black, and cream. His coat was thick and he panted in the valley's heat. Next to his graceful bulk, the foxes seemed small. All three waited until the sound of the shadow herd's iron hooves faded into the distance.

"Well!" The fox Basil sat up and brushed both paws over his pointed muzzle. He sneezed to get the dust raised by the shadow unicorns out of his nose. "That was close."

"Phuut!" Dill, the vixen, snorted at her mate. "They don't even suspect we're here!" Her golden eyes narrowed. She despised the shadow herd with a special hatred.

Basil nuzzled the scar around Dill's neck. She had been a slave of the Shifter's army long ago, before they'd met. That was why they were all here; Dill had been the only animal in Balinor who knew the secret paths through the Valley of Fear. She had led Arianna and the Sunchaser to Castle Entia. Ari and Chase successfully retrieved the Royal Scepter of Balinor. But Ari, Chase, and a third companion, Lori Carmichael, had suddenly disappeared into the Pit. Lincoln, loyal to both Ari and the Sunchaser, refused to leave the Valley of Fear until they were found again.

"We have to go back to the beach on the other side of Demonview," Dill said, resuming the argument they'd been having when the shadow herd suddenly charged through the Fiery Field. "We've got to get back to Balinor."

"Not without Ari," Lincoln said. He trotted to the edge of the Pit. He held his plumy tail low, a sign of worry.

"Stop staring over the edge like that!" Dill whispered crossly. "We'll be discovered!"

Lincoln ignored her. He peered into the depths of the Pit as fruitlessly as before. Late last

11

night, after Ari and Chase had reclaimed the Royal Scepter stolen by the evil Shifter, Kylie the Snake-woman had pushed Arianna, Chase, and Lori Carmichael into the Pit. Lincoln was worried sick. Where were they? When the sun rose that morning, the poor animals and humans who slaved in the Pit and had been recaptured returned to work as usual, guarded by a squad of shadow unicorns. Some of the slaves dug coal out of the sides of the Pit while others filled the carts. Sad-looking oxen dragged the carts from the depths and across the Fiery Field.

Through all this activity, there was no sign of the Princess and the Sunchaser.

"We can't leave without them!" Lincoln said stubbornly.

"What if they aren't here at all?" Dill asked. "You didn't see what happened to them when they fell. I did."

Lincoln growled in frustration. "Tell me again what you saw."

"They fell into a big hole," Dill began.

"What was in the hole?"

"What was in the hole?" Dill asked scornfully. "Dirt, I suppose. It was more like a tunnel than a hole, come to think of it." She squeezed her eyes shut, trying to remember. "Grass. A meadow. And . . . nope!" She shook her head violently. "That's silly. I couldn't have seen that."

"Seen what?" Lincoln asked.

"Unicorns. A herd of ordinary unicorns, like

the regular ones you find all over the place in Balinor, except they didn't have horns."

"Horses!" Lincoln said excitedly.

"Horses?" Dill asked irritably.

"Horses," Lincoln replied. "There aren't any in Balinor. But I know where there are horses."

Dill made a sarcastic noise. Whether this was because she didn't believe in horses or whether she thought Lincoln was crazy, the collie wasn't sure. "Horses," he said patiently. "There are horses at Glacier River Farm. On the other side of the Gap."

"The other side of the Gap!" Dill snorted with amusement. "As if! Nobody lives on the other side of the Gap!"

"I did," Lincoln said. "And Ari lived there for a time, when the Resistance sent her there to keep her from being captured by the Shifter. And Lori Carmichael comes from there."

Dill cocked her head in doubt.

Lincoln backed away from the edge of the Pit, turned around, and sat down, facing both foxes. "If Ari and Chase are on the other side of the Gap we've got work to do," he said grimly. "You're right, Dill. We need to return to the beach and find Captain Tredwell, then sail the *Dawnwalker* back to Sixton. We have to find Tobiano and let him know what's happened."

"Toby." Dill thought about the black-and-white unicorn, then nodded in agreement. "You're right. He'll know what to do."

13

"Why would Toby know what to do?" Basil asked. "We should tell Dr. Bohnes. She's the Princess Arianna's old nurse, and she's got all kinds of connections with the Resistance. She'll know how to get Her Royal Highness and His Majesty, the Sunchaser, back to Balinor."

"You haven't figured it out, Basil," Dill said loftily. "You never figure things out unless I tell you myself. Toby's a Celestial unicorn. He can get word to the Dreamspeaker and Numinor."

"Toby's a Celestial unicorn!" Basil wrinkled his nose, so the black mask around his eyes scrunched up. "He couldn't be."

"Well, he is," Dill said flatly. "He was sent by Atalanta herself to help Her Royal Highness on this quest to the Valley of Fear. So, I say let's go back to the *Dawnwalker,* where Toby's waiting for us! I've been wanting to get out of here for hours!"

Lincoln looked at her gravely. "You two go on ahead."

"What!" cried Dill in dismay.

"I mean it, Dill. This is where Ari and Chase crossed over into the Gap. This is where they'll come out again. I'm not going to leave until they return."

"You're out of your mind, Lincoln." Dill snapped her teeth in irritation. "It's too dangerous here!"

"I won't leave," Lincoln said stubbornly. "And you two should go. Someone has to get word to Tobiano. I'm awfully worried that the Dreamspeaker

14

hasn't contacted us. Something is very wrong in the Celestial Valley. Toby will know how to find Atalanta even when she can't find us. Besides, if we split up, there's a better chance that one of us will sneak through the Shifter's guards and get back to Balinor."

"It does make sense, Dill," Basil said.

"All right," the vixen said crossly. "But you be careful, Lincoln. And as soon as Her Royal Highness and His Majesty come back, you get yourselves back to Balinor! Basil! You roll in the dust to cover up that red coat of yours. Then we're off to find Toby!"

Dill's fur was a mixture of gray, cocoa brown, and dusty white. Here, in the Valley of Fear, where all was dry and dusty, she blended right into the land-scape. Basil's bright red coat was far too conspicu-ous for safety. With a resigned sigh, he rolled vigorously in the dirt. Then he stood up, shook him-self, and looked at Dill hopefully.

"Good enough," she said. "Lincoln? We may not meet again. I will give Captain Tredwell the mes-sage, and then Basil and I will go home, to the Forest of Ardit."

"If we don't get captured by the Shifter," Basil said gloomily.

"Good-bye," Lincoln said. "We never would have gotten this far without you, Dill. We won't for-get you."

"I doubt we'll meet again," Dill said briskly. Then, in a totally un-Dill-like gesture, she licked Lincoln's nose in affection. "Good-bye," she said gruffly. "Take care of yourself."

Basil nodded in agreement. "Watch your back," he advised, giving Lincoln a friendly nudge in farewell. Then the two foxes were off, slipping silently away.

Lincoln suppressed a stab of loneliness. He knew he would never see the two foxes again. With a sigh, he curled into the safety of a thornbush. He settled his nose on his forepaws and kept his eyes on the edge of the Pit. He dozed in the heat in a kind of half sleep.

He woke suddenly, torn from a dream of Glacier River Farm. He had dreamed he was too close to the farmhouse woodstove. He was too hot!

Where was he? He jumped up, disoriented. Ah, yes! The Valley of Fear! The sun had slipped down to the horizon, but it was as hot as ever. The air was thick and still. Perhaps a storm was coming.

Lincoln sniffed the air. Far across the Valley of Fear, the mountain Demonview loomed cold and spare. Darkness rose behind the mountain, blackening the snow. A huge shadow crept over the sky. Lightning split the greasy black clouds. The wind picked up, harsh and hot.

Evil was coming!

Lincoln flattened his ears and whined softly. A giant winged shape rose over Demonview. Its wings beat the air with slow, powerful strokes. The thing flew across the Valley of Fear. Lincoln cowered

16

beneath the bush as it soared overhead. One giant red-rimmed eye peered down from the ghostly head. Lincoln heard the *snap-snap-snap* of a restless beak seeking prey.

Lincoln knew for certain what it was when it flew straight toward Castle Entia: The Shifter had come home.

3

Arianna held out her hand to Lori in a gesture of farewell. She, Lori, and Chase were standing in the south pasture at Glacier River, near the cave that was the entrance to the Gap. Everything was exactly the same as when they had fallen through the Gap and into Balinor two weeks ago. The sun was in the same place in the sky. The white three-board fences surrounded the pasture, where a few horses grazed peacefully. In the distance, Ari could see the gray buildings of the boarding barn and the riding arena. "I guess this is good-bye."

Lori scowled. "What do you mean, good-bye? You have to come and tell my dad what happened to me. He's going to be furious! I've been gone two weeks! I'll bet he's got the police in three states looking for me!"

Ari blinked. This was totally unexpected. No, she decided, it wasn't at all. It was just like Lori to demand that somebody else take care of her problems. "I'm really sorry, Lori, but I can't take the time to do it. Chase and I have to get back to Lincoln and the foxes. We've left them all alone in the Valley of Fear!"

"Tough," Lori said. She folded her arms across her chest and stuck out her lower lip. "You have to help me first."

Ari looked over at Chase. Chase had bent his great bronze head to eat a few mouthfuls of grass. His ebony horn brushed the tops of the clover and alfalfa as he grazed. He was waiting, Ari guessed, for the two girls to figure out how to resolve this.

"I'm sure you can handle your dad," Ari said. "He'll know you couldn't help being away. I mean, all he has to do is look at your clothes!" They were both wearing the black leather uniform of the Shifter's army, the disguises they'd been forced to adopt when they had traveled through the Valley of Fear.

"Forget it," Lori said. "I'm going to be in a lot of trouble, and it wasn't my fault."

Ari shook her head. "Chase and I are going back through the Gap right now, Lori. We've got the Scepter, and we've got to go back over Demonview to the *Dawnwalker*."

"You think you're just going to walk right out of here? Forget it!"

"I'll use the Royal Scepter. I mean, that's why we went to the Valley of Fear. Because of the powerful magic in this." She pulled the Royal Scepter from her belt. It was a heavily carved rosewood staff and very beautiful. It was inlaid with lapis lazuli and the top was an intricately carved unicorn's head. "Now that I have it, Chase and I are going to try to find my mother and father."

"What about MY mother and father?!"

"I'm sure you'll think of something," Ari said helplessly, although she didn't know what it would be. "I'm really sorry, Lori. But I have to go now."

"And you think that thing will help you?" Lori eyed the Scepter scornfully.

"With a little luck, it will." Ari tightened her grip on the Scepter nervously. It had a great deal of powerful magic. She had just begun to learn about it when, on the day of the Great Betrayal, the Scepter was stolen and she and Chase were sent to this side of the Gap by the Resistance. "I have a lot to learn about it still."

Lori rocked back and forth on her heels. Ari wished she would go. Time was valuable. She'd only been gone from the Valley of Fear a few minutes, but she was anxious to get back. "Chase? We should go."

He lifted his head from the grass and gazed somberly at her. "Farewell, Lori. Ari, are you ready to return?"

"We have to try." Ari picked up her leather helmet from the grass and put it back on her head. She held the Scepter up. It didn't look like much at the moment, just a beautifully carved stick with a lovely wooden unicorn head.

"I can't believe you think that thing's going to work," Lori said.

"The Royal Scepter is many things," Chase said, his voice deep and calm. "Sometimes it is a key to open the way to forbidden places. That is how we shall use it now."

"Can you give me a leg up, Lori?" Ari smiled at Chase. She would ride her unicorn through the Gap, holding the Scepter before her.

"You've got to be kidding!"

Ari looked at her soberly. "I won't say 'I'm sorry' again. I've apologized too often. I hope you and your dad won't quarrel about your time in Balinor, Lori." Ari leaped lightly onto Chase's back. She held the Scepter in her right hand, and they rode toward the mouth of the cave. She tucked her chin down as they entered, to avoid hitting her head on the rock ceiling. The Scepter glowed with a faint blue light in the dimness of the cave. Ari and Chase faced the back wall. The cave was gravel, sand, and stone.

Ari held the Scepter out. "Open," she said firmly.

The Scepter grew warm. The wall didn't change.

"Open," Ari said again.

"It's not working," Lori said from behind them. Her voice was unpleasantly triumphant.

"I know it's not working," Ari said a little testily. "Chase?"

"I do not know, milady. I do not understand." He shifted uneasily beneath her. Ari waved the Scepter back and forth. She was beginning to feel a little ridiculous. "I knew being a princess wouldn't be all it's cracked up to be," she muttered under her breath. "We went to all this trouble to get this Scepter back and it won't even . . ."

The back wall exploded in a haze of oily smoke and yellow-green flame! Lori screamed. Chase leaped backward and Ari clutched his mane, clamping her legs tight against his sides. The smoke cleared and the flames died away. A jagged hole gaped where the wall had been.

"Wow," Lori said. She edged her way forward, grabbing at Chase's mane for support. "I don't know if I'd go through there if I were you."

Ari slid off Chase's back and stood next to her. A hideous green light shone from the hole and the air was slimy. Something stunk.

"That smell!" Lori coughed. "It's awful! I don't think you should go in there, Ari. It looks dangerous!"

"Pleeeeasssse! Come innnn."

Ari shuddered. She recognized that hissing voice. Those dry whispery tones. It was the Snakewoman who had pushed them into the Pit!

"Kylie!" Chase said.

Ari swallowed a scream. She grabbed for the

knife in her weapons belt. She could just see the Snakewoman in the sickly green light. Kylie was in her most hideous form — half-woman, half-snake. From the waist down, her body was thick, ropy coils of fungus-mottled white. Her head was human, except for her eyes. They were yellow, and the pupils were black vertical slits. Her hair trailed in greasy lengths around her shoulders.

"Get out of the way," Ari said sternly. "You must let us pass."

Kylie's tongue was red and forked. She lashed out with it and the poisonous tip flicked through the hole, striking Ari's cheek. The pain was intense; Ari's skin burned as if seared by fire. "Try," Kylie said, her voice a creepy parody of welcome. "Jusssst try, human child."

Her face grim, her cheek flaming in pain, Ari drew her knife. Chase moved closer to the Snakewoman. He lowered his horn, the deadly point aimed straight at Kylie's eyes. "Let us pass, Kylie. Or it will be the worse for you."

"I think not, Sunchasssser. No, I think not." She spat. A wall of flames rose behind her and licked at the ceiling. Despite herself, Ari shrank back. She shielded her eyes.

Kylie's thin hiss was triumphant. "I have come to deliver a challenge, Princessss." She made a mockery of the words. "You have upsssset the balance of magic. And for thissss . . . you musssst pay!"

"What do you mean, pay?" Lori asked fearfully. "Pay what?"

"FIRSSSST!" Kylie shouted. "A trial by fire!" The flames around her leaped crazily. "Then! An ordeal by moonlight! And the sign of the challenge will be . . . THISSSS!" With a shriek of fury, she flung herself forward through the hole. She was all snake now, fangs dripping poison, an ugly, scaly skull gleaming in the light of the flames. Her fangs flashed in front of Ari, then sank into the stony floor of the cave.

Two roses sprang up and bloomed in the gloomy light. Kylie breathed a poisonous cloud on the first, a red rose with a long stem and sharp thorns. "Thissss issss the sssign of the firsssst challenge! The trial by fire! And thissss . . ." She spat at the second, a white rose with insects crawling at its faded heart. "Thissss issss the sssign of the ssssecond, the ordeal by moonlight!" She settled back onto her coils, her lipless mouth stretched in a mirthless grin. "Are you ready, Princesssss, for the challengessss?"

"I'm ready for anything," Ari said coldly. She was amazed at how brave she sounded. But this bravery infuriated Kylie. With a hiss of frustration, she darted for Ari's eyes, fangs dripping green venom. Ari cried out and dropped the Scepter. Chase charged forward, his horn piercing the snake's left eye. Kylie screamed. The gouged eye dripped yellow fluid and green blood. She thrashed in the cave, her coiled body whipping the walls. Her tail slashed at the rock, and the roof of the cave began to fall.

Ari felt Lori's hands grab her hair, and then she was being pulled backward. "No!" Ari shouted. "No!" She lunged forward on her hands and knees, gravel and sand falling around her ears. She saw Chase in the dimness, thrusting his horn again and again into the snake. Ari dodged his plunging hooves, scrabbling on the ground for the Scepter, which seemed to find her through the roar of the falling rocks. She held on to the Scepter desperately.

Lori screamed, "Out! Get OUT! The whole thing's caving in!"

Ari stumbled to her feet and grabbed Chase's mane, tugging at it.

Suddenly, all three of them were outside the cave, standing in the safety of the south pasture.

With a thunderous crash the rest of the roof fell in.

The way to the Gap was closed.

The Road to Balinor was blocked!

4

Shaking, Ari wiped the dirt from her eyes and stared at the rubble. She spun around, looking for Chase. He was standing free and unhurt, except for a bloody slash on his withers. Lori sat on the ground, her face white with shock. Ari still clutched the Scepter in one hand. She looked down. The green fire had seared the back of her right hand and a bit of burned blood bubbled up from the wound. The pain was intense.

But the Scepter itself seemed undamaged. She looked it over carefully. The rosewood shaft was unblemished. The inlaid lapis lazuli was unchipped. Even the unicorn's head at the top of the staff was unmarked. Ari rubbed the dust from the gracefully carved head. "Oh, no," she said. She felt very, very tired. "Now what are we going to do?"

"You have two options," the carved unicorn

head said in a clear, tiny voice. "One: Meet the two challenges posed by Lady Kylie, emissary of Entia, the Shifter. Or two: Run away and become someone else altogether."

"Of course it talks," Lori said in exasperation. "I should have expected that."

"It talks," Ari agreed. "Did you hear that, Chase?"

Chase nodded, then sniffed at the Scepter curiously. "I've had no experience with this," he admitted. "It's never said anything before."

"It's very interesting," Ari said. "Maybe it can tell us how to get past that horrible Kylie and back into Balinor." She looked at the unicorn head. It was now mute. "Hello," she said, and shook the Scepter lightly.

The little carved head said nothing.

"Maybe there's a tape recorder in there," Lori suggested. "Unscrew the top and let's see."

Ari grabbed the base of the unicorn's neck and twisted it. The carved wooden eyes rolled up, and the wooden unicorn squeaked, "Stop it!"

"Oh, Chase!" Ari sighed. "What do we do now?"

"You have two options," the unicorn head said. "One: Meet the challenges posed by Lady Kylie, emissary of Entia, the Shifter. Or two: Run away and become someone else altogether."

"You already said that," Lori pointed out.

"Becoming someone else *is* attractive," Ari said. "At least we wouldn't have half-human snakes chasing us. But what are the two challenges?"

"The challenges are invoked when the balance of magic is upset," the unicorn head said. "The first is a trial by fire. The second is an ordeal by moonlight." Its tone was bossy, sounding like a very precise teacher.

"The gross snake-lady told us that already," Lori said. "You're not helping one little bit."

The carved head didn't seem bothered by Lori's rather rude remark, since it didn't respond.

"I think it just answers questions," Ari said thoughtfully. "What is your purpose, um . . ." What should she call it? Your Headness didn't seem very respectful. And it didn't seem like sir or milady was appropriate, either. As a matter of fact, it wasn't like any animal or human she had seen or heard before. "Just what do you do, Scepter?"

"I answer some questions," the carved head responded promptly.

"*Some* questions?" Chase asked. "Not *all* questions?"

"I answer some questions. I do not answer all questions."

"What did I have for dinner last night, then?" Lori asked flippantly.

The Royal Scepter didn't dignify this with a comment of any kind. But its blue lapis eyes flashed in annoyance.

28

Ari thought for a moment, then asked, "What's the difference between the questions you answer and the ones you don't?"

"I am the gatekeeper of the magic beyond magic, Your Royal Highness. There is much you should know about the magic beyond magic. What you *should* know, but do not know, I will tell you."

That sounded reasonable to Ari. "What is the magic beyond magic?" The Scepter looked pleased, then recited in its thin, clear voice:

"Three levels of magic: The first magic is small.
The kind that is done without effort at all.
First magic can turn sweet milk to sour
Or cure stomach upsets or help crops to flower.

The second is mighty and fierce, you will find.
The second belongs to the Dreamspeaker's kind,
And the Shifter, as well, for it helps him disguise
His terrible form from most human eyes.

The third type of magic is deep, not controlled
By humans or those in the unicorns' fold.
Third magic made both the Shifter's dark hand
And Atalanta the Good and her unicorn band.

It begins at the end. It ends at the start.
I guard its gate. The Old Mare is its Heart."

Chase nodded, as if hearing a familiar song or a story told to him many times over.

Ari closed her eyes. A piercing memory came to her: Dr. Bohnes — only she was Bohnesy, her old nurse, and Ari was seven years old at Bohnesy's knee. They sat warm and safe near a fire in the nursery. And Bohnesy recited the poem of the three magics to her, just as the Scepter had done. Tears came to Ari's eyes. She had danced in triumph when she and Chase retrieved the Scepter from Castle Entia. The Scepter was the visible sign of the partnership between them. Now that she had the Scepter back, she and Chase were bonded together in deeper ways than ever before. But the return of the Scepter also meant the return of her memory, just as Atalanta had said it would. Memories were painful. She had lost so much since the day of the Great Betrayal. Her mother. Her father. Her brothers. The throne of Balinor.

Now she had to get it all back.

Ari rubbed her face with one hand. "Then tell us about these two challenges. Do I have to overcome both of them before Chase and I can get back to Balinor?"

"Both of them," the Scepter said a little smugly.

"By fire and by moonlight," Ari mused. "Scepter? Will either of these challenges come on this side of the Gap?"

"The balance of magic was upset on the other side, and to the other side you must return."

"Wait — wait — wait," Lori said. "If you can't

30

return to Balinor until you meet these challenges, and the challenges aren't here, then that thing doesn't make any sense."

"Not all lands on the other side are Balinor," Ari said. "I remember so much now. There are many lands surrounding my country." She raised the Scepter. "Will we go to Rapture-on-the-Sea? Or Fisneth-by-the-Gorge? Is that where the challenges will be?"

"No," the Scepter said.

"I'm getting tired of standing here talking to a stick," Lori complained. "You can settle all this later, Ari. Right now, I want to go home."

"Go on, then," Ari said impatiently. She bit her lip. She didn't have any right to vent her fear and anger at Lori. "I'm sorry. I guess I'm a little scared. I'm just not sure what these challenges are going to mean for Chase and me."

"I told you already. I'm not facing my dad all on my own. It's not my fault you dragged me into the Gap. You practically kidnapped me!"

This was so far from true that Ari didn't even bother to get mad. If Lori hadn't been following Chase, she never would have gotten caught up in the magic that pulled them through the Gap the first time. "Lori," she said gently. "Look at Chase. Just look at him."

Chase gazed straight at Lori. His dark eyes were wrinkled in a smile. His big ebony horn glinted in the clear sunlight. His silky mane flowed over his withers, down to his knees. His long bronze-colored tail brushed the tips of the grass.

"There aren't any unicorns on this side of the Gap," Ari said. "Even if I left him here, hidden, someone from your world is bound to find him — and then where would we be? Chase and I have to use the Scepter to get back to Balinor *right now*. If we stay much longer in the south pasture, a human from this side of the Gap is going to discover us both."

Lori's face reddened. "You don't get it, do you?" she demanded. "I can't just go home without an explanation. My dad will kill me."

"I think he'll be so happy to see you and relieved that you're safe that he won't be angry. And if he is, it won't last very long."

"So you won't help me?"

"I can't, Lori. I would if I could. But the risk to Chase is too great. Now listen to me." She smiled a little. "Make sure you go into the tack room and the barn and change out of that black leather uniform you're wearing. You'll have a hard time explaining why you're in that getup."

Lori turned her back to all of them: unicorn, Princess, and Royal Scepter. Ari could tell she was crying — crying hard. She must be terrified of her father.

Chase pawed the ground. "We'd better hurry, milady. We've left Lincoln and the foxes alone too long. I'm beginning to worry."

Ari nodded. She bit her lip, then walked up to Lori and put her hand on her shoulder. Lori shrugged her off. Ari's own eyes prickled in response to Lori's tears. How terrible to be so afraid of your father!

"Lori?"

No answer.

"Despite — despite everything, I'm really glad you were with us. And I'm going to miss you."

Lori flipped her hair back and scrubbed her face with her hands.

Ari exchanged a long look with Chase. He shook his head slightly. He was right. There was nothing Ari could do. Sometimes being a Princess meant making very hard choices.

Ari held the Scepter up to the sunlight. "Scepter? Can Chase and I cross the Gap?"

"Yes."

"Will the Snakewoman be waiting for us? Or any of the Shifter's army?" Her hand went to the knife in her weapons belt. If they were, she would fight!

"No," the Scepter said cheerily. "You will not engage the Shifter or any of his followers until the first challenge."

"How do we cross over, Scepter?"

The wooden unicorn head swiveled on the shaft. Its blue lapis eyes fixed on the entrance to the cave. Several large boulders blocked the way. A slide of dirt and gravel was packed around them. "You have two options. One: Dig the opening free."

"I hope the other one is easier," Ari said. "Digging would take quite a while."

"Or two: Use magic."

"I'd prefer to use magic."

"Humph," said the Scepter disapprovingly. "Always the easy way. All right. You must mount the unicorn and ride straight toward the opening. And don't let go of me," the Scepter scolded as Chase knelt down to allow Ari to mount. "I'll be moving a lot of dirt here, and I need to concentrate."

Ari jumped on Chase, held the Scepter out, and guided Chase with her knees. He trotted slowly toward the cave, and as he trotted, the Scepter began to glow, radiating a green-blue light, like the waters of a tropical beach. The glow ran down Ari's arm over her back and along Chase's sides. There was a moment — short, astonishing — in which Ari and Chase were one being, unicorn and girl fused into a single figure with two minds existing side by side. Ari could see, hear, and taste just as Chase did! She marveled at the way the ground felt under his hooves, at the messages that came to him from the scents in the wind, the shift of light!

So this was what the Bonded Magic was like!

The magic swelled, a great chorus of sound and light. Ari and Chase rode forward as one being, the Scepter a steady beacon lighting their way. The boulders shook and rumbled. Dirt and gravel trickled from the top of the pile like a waterfall, moving faster and faster. Dirt swept in great waves from the sides of the boulders, rising around Chase's hocks, releasing fine grit into the air, choking them both.

Ari shut her eyes against the spray of dirt. Chase moved steadily forward, and she did her best to hold the Scepter high.

The blue light flared a tidal wave of brilliance washing the dirt aside. The ground trembled beneath their feet. With a final thunderous roar, the boulders cascaded into the clearing.

The dust settled. It was very quiet.

"Humph!" the Scepter said in a pleased way.

The path to the other side was open.

5

Atalanta made her way wearily to the Watching Pool. Arianna and the Sunchaser were still missing. Each day for the past two weeks she had climbed the rocky path to the magic water. Each day she had been disappointed. Still no visions came to her of Balinor or the world beyond the Gap.

She bent her lovely head; three times her crystal horn touched the water. Three times she called Arianna's name.

Nothing. The mirror to the world below was blank.

Restlessly she paced up and down the path beside the pool. Then a familiar black-and-white shape picked its way through the trees. Tobiano, the sturdy unicorn who had acted as her emissary to Balinor, had returned that morning. He had already told Atalanta that the foxes Basil and Dill came back with a terrible tale of Arianna's disappearance. The two of them, and Lincoln, had waited in vain for Her Royal Highness to return. Basil and Dill had returned from the Valley of Fear and sailed on the *Dawnwalker* back to Sixton. They found Toby waiting as he had promised. Toby listened, then made his way from Sixton to the path to the Celestial Valley.

Atalanta had sent him off to graze; she was a little surprised to see him return so soon.

"Hello, Toby," she said. "Have you rested well?" Her voice was soft and as musical as ever.

But the stout unicorn noted her tired eyes and the slump to her withers. "You look terrible," he said in his blunt, rude way. "I brought someone to cheer you up. Lincoln, tell the Dreamspeaker what you've just told me."

He stepped aside. Atalanta's violet eyes widened in astonishment. Arianna's collie, Lincoln, stood there. He was thin, his coat was ragged and dirty, and his white forepaws were stained with blood. He had come a long way. But what amazed Atalanta was not his pitiful condition. She was shocked to see him here at all — in the Celestial Valley, where no beings but the Celestial unicorns were allowed.

These were indeed strange days! The balance of magic was having a greater effect than anyone could tell.

"Welcome, Lincoln," she said.

The dog looked at her and bowed before her. "I never thought I would speak to you, Dream-speaker," he said. "I am the most fortunate of dogs!"

"I found him at the gateway to Balinor," Toby said. "I was grazing that little patch of four-leaf clover around the Crystal Arch and I heard this scratching and whining, so I turned the lock in the door with the tip of my horn, and ha! There he was." He looked down at the dog. "Looks awful," he observed. "Must have been on a hard journey, wherever he's been. I've never known an animal or human from the world below to make that journey."

Atalanta lifted her head and gazed up at the sun. She sent a silent thanks upward. Magic strong enough to allow this dog to visit the Celestial Valley was the work of the Old Mare of the Mountain. Atalanta rejoiced, but her heart was filled with fear. The Old Mare of the Mountain was not one to hand out favors. Events must be more perilous than Atalanta had thought.

"Are you hungry, Lincoln?" she asked in her gentle voice. "And have you had water to drink?"

"He has *news*, Dreamspeaker," Toby burst out. "He has no time for food or water!"

"His news will do us no good if he is faint from hunger and exhaustion," Atalanta said.

Lincoln rose stiffly to his feet. His dark brown eyes were worried. "I will not eat or drink, milady, until I tell you what I know. You must save Arianna! There is no one else to help!"

"Then tell me," Atalanta said. "I, too, am concerned about Her Royal Highness and the Sunchaser."

"As Toby told you, I waited by the Pit for Ari and Chase. While I waited . . ."Lincoln shivered, as if a frigid wind hit him. "*He* returned."

"Entia, the Shifter," Toby said, as if this weren't perfectly obvious to the Dreamspeaker.

"He came back as a giant bird. His wings covered the Valley of Fear. He flew straight to Castle Entia. He summoned his army to him. All the shadow unicorns left the Pit at his command. Then, for half a day, all was quiet."

The dog flattened his ears. Atalanta noted that one of his eyeteeth was broken. "And then, a great cloud of fire and oily smoke flared up from the Palace towers. The herd of shadow unicorns poured out from the gates! A giant unicorn stallion led them, the largest I've ever seen! It breathed fire! Lightning crackled from his iron horn . . ." Lincoln stopped and shivered.

"Moloth," Atalanta said. "Herd leader of the shadow unicorns. And on his back, Lincoln?"

"Yes," Lincoln said. "The Shadow Rider. I hid in the thornbushes by the Pit. The unicorn army swept by me and thundered into the Pit! There was a flash of green fire . . . and the Shadow Rider was gone! I am afraid . . . I am very afraid . . ."

39

"That the Shadow Rider has been sent to attack the Princess and the Sunchaser," Atalanta said. "Yes. The first challenge is trial by fire. And with the Royal Scepter gone, the Shifter has the right to force the trial. There is Deep Magic in the Scepter, Lincoln. Part of this magic keeps the barrier between our world and the next. I wonder . . ." Her violet eyes were half closed. "I wonder if the Scepter's absence is one of the reasons you were able to come to us here in the Celestial Valley. I also wonder . . ."

"What, Dreamspeaker?" Toby demanded.

Atalanta's glance at him was slightly reproving. Tobiano was indeed the rudest unicorn in the Celestial Valley herd — although he had a loyal heart. "I will keep my own counsel, Tobiano. You have done well, both of you. Perhaps I, too, can use this temporary imbalance to send some help." She shook her head and her silky mane swirled around her withers. "And then again, perhaps not. All I can do is try." She turned her grave violet eyes on the collie. "Lincoln, you have made a noble journey. If you eat and drink of the food we have here in the Celestial Valley, you will forget this time with me. You will forget what I have told you."

"Then I cannot eat or drink, Dreamspeaker. I must return to my mistress and tell her all that I know."

Atalanta nodded. She wheeled suddenly. Her crystal horn glittered like the rarest jewel ever seen.

"Toby," she said. "Please take Lincoln and show him the path back to the Fiery Field. I have work to do." She walked over the rise.

Lincoln followed her glowing violet light with his eyes until she disappeared.

6

The way through the Gap had been opened by the Scepter. Ari hesitated for only a moment. Behind her were the sunny fields and pastures of Glacier River. Ahead, the dark depths loomed.

She and Chase had to pass through.

The Scepter had told her that the Shifter's followers would leave them alone until the first challenge, but she drew her knife, just in case. She tapped her heels lightly against Chase's flanks. Chase walked forward.

She held up the Scepter. The steady blue light narrowed to a single beam. It illuminated the rocky floor of the cave. Chase's hooves rang against the rocks. Every nerve in Ari's body was alert. The path twisted and wound through what was no longer a cave but a tunnel. The roof vaulted high above them. It was eerily quiet, the silence broken only by the dripping of water somewhere off to the right, and the soft shuffle of small animals in the crevices.

"Scepter, can you give us more light?" Ari whispered.

"Yes."

The narrow beam didn't change. Ari bit her lip in exasperation. The Scepter appeared to be very literal-minded. She'd have to remember that.

"Scepter, would you please broaden the light?"

The blue light spread out like seeping water, illuminating the sides of the tunnel. Ari was so shocked at what she saw that she brought Chase to a halt.

Wooden doors lined the tunnel walls! There were many of them, all constructed of broad planks, all with arched tops. The hinges and latches were made of black iron. "Where do these doors lead to?" Ari asked.

"Other countries," the Scepter said. "Other lands. None of them Balinor, Your Royal Highness."

"We need to press on," Chase said. He moved out, without her permission.

Someday, Ari thought, *when all of this is over, I will return here if I can.* She would love a chance to explore new lands.

The path sloped up. The tunnel narrowed. After a few more paces, Ari had to bend over Chase's neck to avoid scraping her head on the roof. Chase came to a halt where the tunnel ended abruptly —

a space so narrow that Ari's legs brushed against the walls. The way out was at the end of a short, steep incline. She could just make out the opening above her. When she and Chase had left the Pit in the Valley of Fear, it had been night. It was night still. She could smell the desert air and see a huge yellow moon far above in the sky.

Something about the moon bothered her. She narrowed her eyes and stared at it.

She urged Chase on. He scrambled up the incline, hindquarters bunched, plunging up and down.

"Would you please shut off your light, Scepter?" Ari asked in a low voice. "We may be seen by the Shifter's guards."

The blue light went off, and Ari was in a darkness so profound she gasped. She waited a moment for her eyes to adjust, then urged Chase on. With a last powerful leap, they were out of the Gap, and onto the floor of the Pit.

Ari reined Chase in and peered into the night. The scent of burning fire and ash was horribly familiar. The moon hung like an overripe fruit in the sky.

The moon. Ari frowned. At most, they'd been in Glacier River half an hour. No more. There had been no moon when she and Chase had followed Lori through the Gap. It had been a Shifter's Moon, when the moon itself was dark. Now it was full!

Her heart pounding with worry, she and

Chase made their way up the narrow trail to the top of the Pit. They passed abandoned carts, half-filled with the stones the slaves of the Pit hauled back and forth at the whim of the Shifter. Small animals stirred in the night. Ari kept her hand on her knife, afraid to disturb the sinister darkness with questions to the Scepter. She sent her thoughts to Chase. *This doesn't look right.*

It does not, he agreed.

They came out of the Pit to a desolate landscape. The Fiery Field stretched beyond the Pit, pocked by circles of dim red flames. The scrubby brush surrounding the Pit was just as Ari remembered. "Basil? Dill?" she whispered. "Linc! Lincoln!"

Nothing stirred. Ari slipped off Chase's back. The place looked deserted. If the Shifter's followers were here, they were well concealed. She pulled the Scepter from her weapons belt and addressed it softly. "Scepter! Where is my dog?"

The blue light illuminated the surrounding dark like a beacon. Ari thrust it under her coat. "The dog is asleep in the brush, thirty paces to the north of where you are standing," the Specter mumbled. "And I don't like it under here!"

"Then turn yourself off," Ari said in a low voice.

The light winked out.

North, Ari thought to herself. Which way was north? Ari looked up at the sky. The stars in the Valley of Fear shone dimly, veiled by the miasma of oily smoke. But she found Callista, the North Star, right where it ought to be. Ari counted off thirty paces, Chase walking gravely behind her. She stopped at a thick stand of thornbush. "Lincoln," she whispered. "Linc!"

A low whine, a muffled bark of greeting. The collie crawled from beneath the brush, his tail wagging feebly. His coat was matted with burrs and his little white forepaws were stained with blood. Ari dropped to her knees, tears stinging her eyes. She cradled the dog's muzzle in her hands. "Hey, boy," she said softly. "Hey!"

"Milady," Lincoln said. "You're back!" He struggled to his feet. He nudged her affectionately.

Ari ran her hands down his sides. She could feel his ribs. "When did you last eat, Linc?" she asked. She kept her voice steady and calm. She rubbed the tips of his ears lightly. "Quite a while ago, I should think." Her lips trembling, she urged him to lie down. One hand on his head, she fumbled at her belt. He needed the first magic, the magic of Dr. Bohnes, her old nurse. And she had that magic — along with the Star Bottle given to her by Atalanta — right at her fingertips.

"A small magic," Dr. Bohnes had said when she'd given Ari the leather bag so many adventures ago. "Use it when you have need."

And there is need now! Ari thought desperately. She opened the little bag and shook its contents onto the dirt. A small bowl. An even smaller package wrapped in paper, and a few other odds and ends. Ari set the bowl upright. She drew the Scepter from underneath her jacket. She now remembered how to use the first magic, the magic that had been given to her and to Chase when they were bonded so long ago. She remembered all that she'd forgotten during the dark days when she had been Ari Langley, stable hand at Glacier River farm, with broken legs and no memory.

She was Arianna, High Princess of Balinor. And she was going to save her dog. "By Callista and Caliman," she said, her hands cupped in midair over the bowl. "I ask for water on behalf of one who is much beloved."

For that was the key to the first magic. You couldn't use it for yourself. It had to be used to do good for others.

She opened her hands. Water filled the pottery bowl. Lincoln lifted his head, and despite his stoic attempts at bravery, he whined eagerly. Ari moved the bowl to his muzzle, and he drank deeply.

She unwrapped the square package and spread the cloth on the sand. She held her hands over it. "By Bandon and Barr, I ask for food on behalf of one who is much beloved."

She settled back on her heels. Lincoln drained the water bowl three times, then gulped the food. The magical food and water worked fast. His eyes brightened. His ribs filled out. He looked at her with love and devotion in his deep brown eyes, and attacked a fourth serving of food with zest.

"Well," sniped a familiar voice behind her. "Looks like you can do magic, too!"

Ari jumped and whirled, her knife at the ready without conscious thought. "Lori!" she shouted. "What are you doing here?"

Lori stood defiantly in the moonlight.

"She followed us," Chase said. "I was so intent on getting us through the Gap safely, I didn't notice. I discovered her hiding by the gate to the Gap a few moments ago."

"And I'm not going back," Lori said. She crossed her arms over her leather jacket and scowled. "Not until you come with me."

"Are you crazy?" Ari gasped. "Do you know what danger I have to face, and soon? Lori! Go back! Go back while there's still . . . !"

"THERE THEY ARE!"

Ari froze. Shadow unicorns! The Fiery Field was suddenly alive with the thrum of iron hooves and the glow of their red eyes!

Chase reared and whinnied a challenge. He threw himself in front of Ari and lowered his horn in threat. The shadow unicorns surrounded them, flames curling from their muzzles, iron horns pointed at Chase's bronze chest. The leader advanced his head at a cocky angle, a sneer in his flaming eyes.

"Moloth!" Lincoln growled. He bared his teeth. He came to Ari's side.

"Moloth!" Chase said. "Advance on me at your own peril!"

Moloth shifted his weight to his hindquarters, ready to charge. He was huge and powerfully built, with a thickly muscled neck. His iron horn had been sharpened to a deadly point. His herdmates jostled behind him, their eager whinnies a threatening rumble. "You have something that belongs to my master," he said silkily. "Give it back, and we will let you go."

Ari stepped forward, the Royal Scepter in her hand. The blue light glowed brightly. The shadow herd drew back, muttering fearfully. "I am Arianna, Princess of Balinor," she said. "I carry the Royal Scepter! It belongs to me and the Royal House of Balinor! I have retrieved it from this place!"

"You stole it!" Moloth grated. "From my master! And I demand it back!"

"It was not the Shifter's to begin with!" Ari said. "It was obtained through treachery!"

"And you took it across the Gap!" Moloth said. "The balance of magic must be restored! We shall settle this!" He pawed at the ground. His evil eyes glowed.

"But not here. And not now," Chase said. "You know the rules, Moloth. Will you trespass now?" He surged forward eagerly. He despised the Shifter's herd leader with a special hatred. "For if you do, we shall fight! To the Final Death!"

Ari put her hand on Chase's neck. He quieted under her touch. But she could feel the throb of the great muscles under her hand. "We will meet again at the appointed time, Moloth," she said sternly. "Even you cannot flout the Deep Magic." She held up the Scepter. "Scepter! What shall Moloth do?"

"You have two options," the unicorn head said. Its voice was tinny in the dry desert air. "One: You can charge Her Royal Highness and His Majesty and try to squash them flat. Or two: You can give them safe conduct out of the Valley of Fear."

Ari suppressed a desire to give the Scepter a good thwack. It wasn't the Scepter's fault that the Deep Magic always offered choices, without regard to the consequences. But you never knew about beings like Moloth. Sometimes they took the wrong option just because they were evil and didn't care about consequences.

But if nothing else, Moloth's fear of his master, the Shifter, was greater than his desire to maim and kill.

Chase, who hadn't taken his eyes off Moloth for a second, rumbled, "Safe conduct to the slopes of Demonview, Moloth. Or you die here and now."

Moloth rolled his lips back from his teeth. Ari and her little band were outnumbered three to one. It wouldn't be Moloth who would die here in the Fiery Field, and the black unicorn knew it. But his master had demanded the first challenge — a trial by fire! He reared and screamed at them, a wordless bellow of hate.

"Chase," Ari said quietly. "Kneel so that I can mount."

The great bronze unicorn trembled, but he knelt for her to mount. Ari slipped onto his back.

Lori whimpered.

"Go back now, Lori." Ari didn't take her eyes off Moloth and his herdmates. They crowded together in the darkness, their red eyes glowing. "Go back while you can!"

"I'm afraid!" Lori was crying so hard her voice was a mere thread. "I can't go back by myself! They'll come after me!"

Ari forced herself to look into Moloth's fiery eyes. It was true. He and the shadow unicorns would chase Lori through the Gap. And because the balance of magic had been upset, they might very well get through!

"Get up behind me, then. On Chase. Hang on to my belt."

Lori clambered up Chase's side and onto his back. The unicorn rose easily to his feet. He could take four times the weight of the two girls without any problem.

"Go now," Moloth hissed at them. "But we shall meet again. And soon!"

Ari tapped Chase with her heels. He sprang

into a long, easy canter. Lincoln ran silently at his flank. Lori shifted her weight and clutched Ari's weapons belt.

That trip through the darkness to the slopes of Demonview seemed to take hours. But Chase never faltered. They ran through the night and the Royal Scepter lit the way. Chase leaped over the ashy pits of fire, dropped to a walk quickly through the Fiery Path. Lincoln bounded ahead of them, uttering no whine of complaint. Ari bit her lip when she caught the scent of singed fur as her collie raced through the coals.

They would make it through the Fiery Field to the snow-covered flanks of the mountain. They had made their way over Demonview through a terrible blizzard, so Ari was certain they could make their way back. They had the Scepter now. And Ari had regained command of the first magic.

They would make it to the shore of the Sixth Sea. She knew that. But there was one thing she didn't know. And it haunted those dark hours as they struggled to the safety of the shore.

What had happened to the time? She had been at Glacier River for less than half an hour. And yet, Lincoln had waited for her by the Pit — a wait that had been long and terrible. He hadn't lost all that weight in half an hour. And the moon was now full. It had been the Shifter's Moon before, a night of no moon at all.

What was going on?

Captain Tredwell and his ship, the *Dawn-walker*, should be waiting to take them home to Balinor. She had left instructions they should wait three days but she *knew* more than three days had passed here.

Would the captain be there?

The night wore on. They struggled up the side of Demonview, snow whirling about them, freezing their fingers and toes. They reached the summit, paused for a brief rest, then plunged down again.

They reached the other side as the sun rose in the east, flooding the calm waters of the Sixth Sea with warm and welcome light.

Ari sat on Chase and looked desperately up and down the coastline as they made their way to the beach.

The *Dawnwalker* wasn't there.

7

Ari sat at the water's edge. Her boots were off, and she wriggled her toes in the cool sand. She was exhausted from the trek through the Valley of Fear, and so were the others. Lincoln lay curled up nearby, his nose tucked into the end of his white plumy tail. He had told her of his trip to the Celestial Valley, and Ari was comforted. She trusted the Dreamspeaker. And if Atalanta were going to send help, it would come eventually . . . if the Deep Magic allowed her to send help.

Lori sat with her legs drawn up, knees on her chin. She gazed moodily into space.

Only Chase seemed unfazed by their labors. He stood where the grass met the sandy beach, gazing out to sea. Ari got to her feet and went to him. "I don't understand about the time," she admitted. "I asked Lincoln where Basil and Dill went. He said they left for the *Dawnwalker* two weeks ago! But

Chase, we were only in Glacier River for a short time. What happened?"

"Approximately fifteen and a half minutes have passed on the other side of the Gap compared to two weeks, one day, and four hours in Balinor," the Scepter said from Ari's weapons belt. "This is a function of the time-space slip that occurred ten thousand years ago when Balinor split off from . . ."

Ari closed her hand firmly around the unicorn head to shut it up. "Do you mean," she said after a stunned moment, "that time is not the same on the other side of the Gap?"

"Time," the Scepter mused. "Time is not the same anywhere." Afraid of a long and confusing lecture on the nature of time, Ari said thank-you politely and tucked the Scepter away. "Wow," she said. Then, "Poor Lori!"

"She would have been able to return to the farm with no one the wiser," Chase agreed.

"Scepter?" Ari brought the Scepter out again.

"I'm sleeping!" the Scepter retorted.

"You can go back to sleep in a second," Ari said. "A second of Balinor time."

"Ha-ha," the Specter said grouchily.

"Where are Basil and Dill? Are they all right?"

"In the Forest of Ardit, chasing voles. Dill will have a cub in the spring. Basil remains henpecked."

Ari took a deep breath, trying to think of the next question. It was very difficult dealing with a Scepter that would only answer a direct question.

There was so much she needed to know! And so little time! "Does Atalanta know where we are?"

"No."

"Will the Watching Pool send her visions of us, as it has before? And if not, why not," Ari added hastily.

"The Watching Pool is dark. When you took me out of Balinor, you upset the balance of magic. You must meet the two challenges to restore the balance. Then the Watching Pool will clear."

"How much depends on these two challenges?" Ari asked but she was pretty sure she didn't want to know the answer.

"There are many possibilities. One: You will fail the challenges and the Watching Pool will remain forever dark. Or two: You will not be able to resume your place as High Princess of Balinor. Or three: Lori will not be able to return through the Gap to her own time and place. Four —"

"That's enough," Ari said shortly. And it was. She didn't need to know any more. Everything depended on her beating the Shifter!

"Milady!"

Ari's heart leaped at the excitement in Chase's voice.

He turned to her. His bronze mane whipped around his neck in the stiff ocean breeze. "Do you see it?" he called. "On the horizon! The white sails of the *Dawnwalker!*"

Ari went to stand beside him. The ship was

on the horizon, sailing straight for them. The hull was deep green and she could even see the beautiful figurehead of the star of the morning on its prow. She could just barely pick out the gold letters that spelled the ship's name.

Lincoln woke at Chase's shout and ran up and down the shoreline, barking happily.

The ship soon sailed into the harbor and anchored offshore. Ari waved at Captain Tredwell on the deck. He waved back, then climbed down the rope ladder on the ship's side to get into the dinghy. He brought two sailors with him: a round, chubby man with a little fringe of beard whom Ari recognized as First Mate Quire, and another sailor to row the boat.

The reunion was happy. Captain Tredwell helped Ari, Lori, and Lincoln into the dinghy. Chase leaped into the waves and swam with them. In no time at all, Ari was sitting with Quire and Captain Tredwell in the captain's cabin.

"I got quite a turn, seeing you in that Shifter's army uniform, milady," Quire said shyly.

"It worked well as a disguise," Ari said. She glanced down at herself. The leather was torn and incredibly dirty. She wanted a bath and a change of clothes. Lori and Linc were both getting cleaned up, but Ari wouldn't see to her own needs until she knew what was going on. "Tell me the news, Captain."

"We know what happened, of course, Your

Royal Highness," Captain Tredwell said. His bright gray eyes looked brilliant in the tan of his face. He scratched his brown beard thoughtfully. "Tobiano showed up dockside a few days ago, and gave me orders from Atalanta. I am to take you where you need to go."

"I'm not sure I know where," Ari said ruefully. "I had no idea that taking the Royal Scepter out of Balinor would cause such trouble. I didn't mean to do it. I came through the Gap right after Lori and when I tried to return using the Scepter to open the way . . ." She swallowed. Kylie's slitted yellow eyes would haunt her for a long time to come. "Anyway, one of the Shifter's creatures barred the way."

"We should have been there to help you!" Quire said. "We are supposed to be here to protect you!"

"How could you know what was happening?" Ari looked at them both with affection. So many people had risked their lives to help her. When the Resistance sent Chase and Ari to Glacier River to hide them from the Shifter, the Palace servants Anale and Franc had come along to act as her guardians and foster parents. They had both been servants of Ari's father, the King. But Captain Tredwell and Quire had no real reason to come to her aid — except that they were loyal subjects. And now she was going to have to involve them in the dangers ahead. "Entia, the Shifter, has issued two challenges. Do you know anything about it?"

"Two challenges?" Captain Tredwell said. "I have no idea, Your Royal Highness. Tobiano just said that we were to take you where you needed to go."

"A trial by fire and an ordeal by moonlight," Ari recalled. "And I'm to recognize the challenge by two roses."

The captain shook his head. "I don't know, milady. But the ship and I stand ready to aid you in any way we can."

Ari nodded. She would have to trust in Atalanta. So they all would have to wait. "Thank you, Captain. The first thing I want to do is get out of this uniform and wash my hair. Perhaps we can talk over dinner."

"It will be ready when you are, milady."

Ari bade them farewell and went out onto the deck. The sea air was fresh and cold. The *Dawnwalker* rocked peacefully at anchor on the waves.

The moon rode high and white in a cloudless sky. A few stars hung in lonely splendor. Ari made her way to the cabin she had shared with Lori on their journey out to Demonview.

Lori was asleep in the hammock. Ari looked at her. She hadn't yet told Lori that she didn't need to be afraid to go back to Glacier River. That time was different here in Balinor. She rubbed her eyes. So many decisions! But she couldn't do everything at once. She would have to wait until the two challenges were over to help Lori get back to Glacier

River. Until then, there was no way for her to get to the Dreamspeaker to ask for help.

"Sorry again," she said softly to the sleeping girl. "But I'll help you get back, Lori. I promise."

Ari washed, using the pitcher and basin one of the sailors had set out for her. Then she changed into her own clothes: the long red skirt with the embroidered hem, the soft blouse and vest, and her comfortable leather boots. She tucked her father's knife in her right boot, laced her leather vest up snugly, then stood with the Scepter in her hand. Where to keep it, for safety's sake? She took some rawhide and tied it around her waist, then looped the long end around the Scepter. It hung to her knees, hidden in the folds of her skirt.

She made her way back to the deck. The lights in the captain's cabin shone with welcoming warmth. Ari walked to the door, knocked, and went in.

The captain and Quire were seated at the large round table he used as a desk. It had been set for dinner with dishes from Balinor. Ari slid into her chair and looked at the cups and plates. They were blue and white, painted with figures of the lords and ladies of the King's Court. Ari recognized Dr. Bohnes, dressed in formal Court attire, her expression lively and alert. And the young Prince next to her was Ari's brother Bren. Tears prickled in Ari's eyes. She ran her thumb over his painted face.

"It's hard to remember," Quire said softly. "Have courage, milady."

"I miss my brothers," Ari said. Her legs ached — a sudden and unwelcome reminder of the terrible injuries she'd sustained on the day of the Great Betrayal. "I haven't seen them since the day the Shifter took over the Palace." She blinked back tears.

The captain looked at Bren's face on the plate with stern affection. "His Royal Highness. I remember him so well, milady. They say you and he used to play at sword fighting in the great courtyard. You must miss those times."

"Yes." Ari drove her hands through her hair to press away the memories. Then she put her hands flat on the table, and said firmly, "No more, Captain. I won't look back. I'll look forward from here on." She accepted a dish of fish and vegetables from Quire and began to eat hungrily. She was starved. She felt as if she hadn't eaten for weeks. "I can't think about the past now. It will make me too sad. And there is too much to do. I don't have any time for grief." She swallowed hard, choking a little on the food. "But I do miss them. My mother. My father. All of them. And I will regain the throne, Captain."

"I hope so, milady." The captain's face was gray with worry. He bit his lip, then slid a folded piece of paper across the table to Ari. "But we'll have to get through this first. While you were freshening up, a great black bird landed on the forecastle. It carried this in its beak."

Curious, Ari unfolded the paper. At first glance, it appeared to be an announcement for a unicorn race. It looked brutal: twenty jumps over a three-mile course. The smallest of the jumps was four-feet-six in height and the highest was close to six feet. Many of the jumps looked strange. She blinked. Were the jumps over pits of fire? "To be held in Deridia," she read aloud. "Where is Deridia?"

Captain Tredwell frowned. "A half day's sail from here. South by southeast. Or so the charts say. I have never been there. And there is a very good reason, Your Royal Highness. The Shifter's forces almost wholly occupy it. It is one of his strongholds. It is a land of heat and fire, they say. Unwelcoming and cruel."

Ari looked at the end of the announcement.

Her hands grew cold.

A red rose was inscribed at the bottom. The thorns were sharp and long. The leaves were mottled with black mold. The heart of the red rose was infected with a disease leaving black spots and cankers on the petals.

She set the paper down. "Well," she said, her mouth dry. "This is it, then. The trial by fire."

Quire nodded. "I'm afraid it is. The first challenge. You and His Majesty, the Sunchaser, will have to ride the steeplechase tomorrow. And you will have to win."

8

Deridia was a town of despair and decay. The sun was a hot bronze hammer on the flat water of the harbor. Garbage floated on the tide and the air was hazy with the smoke from slow-burning pits of coal.

The *Dawnwalker* was able to sail right up to the dock. As Captain Tredwell said, the only advantage the dried-up city had was its deepwater harbor.

Ari and Chase stood at the stern of the *Dawnwalker* and surveyed the buildings before them. Those near the wharf were tumbledown sheds. Tired-looking men and women dragged themselves around the streets; most simply sat, their backs against the walls, and gazed at the *Dawnwalker* with incurious eyes.

Except for the soldiers who rode black unicorns through the cobblestone streets.

They were not the unicorns of the shadow

herd from the Fiery Field, but sad brothers to the unicorns of Balinor. They were Chase's subjects — or had been, before the Shifter had subjugated them. They moved as if they were old, tired, dispirited slugs, their hard iron hooves clattering mournfully. The soldiers who rode them were full of energy and menace. All Ari could see of their faces were their eyes, glittering behind the iron grills of their helmets, since they were dressed in black leather from head to toe.

Posters were mounted at intervals on the walls of the shacks and huts.

Chase's keen eyes narrowed.

"Can you read them?" Ari asked.

"The posters announce the competition. Tomorrow morning, on the west side of this place. The course begins at the town hall and fans out toward those low mountains. It seems to be through the burned-out coal mines."

"Does it say that this is the first challenge?" Lori asked. She squinted. "I can barely see the letters."

"No," Chase said. "Merely that this is a race for the honor and glory of Entia, the Shifter. It demands that challengers register with the town clerk."

"We had better do that, then," Ari said with a sigh. She took the Scepter from the folds of her skirt. She held it and addressed the wooden head. "Scepter? Am I to enter this race as Arianna, Princess of Balinor?"

The Scepter's blue light was thin and pale in this harsh land. "No," the Scepter said bluntly.

"Then who am I?"

"Your throne is in jeopardy," the Scepter said crossly. "And there are enemies all around you. The challenges are known to you and your closest advisors and to the Shifter and his intimate circle. So you have two options . . ."

Lori groaned.

"One: Appear as your true self, Arianna, Princess of Balinor, Bonded to His Majesty, the Sunchaser. The odds are two to one that some follower of Entia will try to poison you in your bed tonight. Entia has taught them to fear you. Or two: Appear as Ari, friend of the people, with the last of the Royal unicorns from the House of Balinor's stables. No ordinary person can win against the Shifter's forces, so you'll be spared because they will want to see the humiliation of your defeat."

"Nice people," Lori commented.

Ari ordered Captain Tredwell, Quire, and the rest of the men to stay on board the ship. "Because we may have to make a run for it, if Chase and I lose," she said soberly. "I need to know that you are here, and that you can get us away safely."

"We will not leave you, Your Royal Highness," Captain Tredwell said. He stood at the helm of the *Dawnwalker*, his eyes keen in his deeply tanned face.

"You must, if something happens to Chase or me," Ari said softly. "I command it."

He looked at her sadly. "I hear and obey, Your Royal Highness."

Ari, Lincoln, Lori, and Chase descended the gangplank cautiously in single file. They walked through the streets of Deridia, seeing the poverty, the dirt, and the despair.

We must save them from this, milady! Chase thought at her. *The Shifter's army set the coal mines on fire when they attacked this place. No one has been able to put them out.*

"We must overcome the first challenge," she responded. "And the second. Then we will sweep all of this before us, and restore happiness to this place." Ari stopped at the decrepit village hall and registered for the race. The apathetic clerk pushed the entry papers at her, and she folded them into her skirt pocket.

They found a small Inn on the edge of town, near the field where the race was to be held. The Innkeeper and his wife were as quiet and repressed as the rest of the people she'd seen in Deridia. The Innkeeper's name was Soltin. He was a compact man, with the powerful build of a blacksmith. His wife, Sola, was solemn. Her hair was wrapped neatly in a kerchief, and she kept her hands folded and her head down when Ari asked for one room and a large stall for Chase. Sola raised her head and looked at the unicorn. Her brown eyes gleamed for a moment as she took in his alert eyes and magnificent head. She looked sharply at Ari and then said in a casual way, "And where are you from, milady?"

66

"We have traveled from Sixton," Ari said truthfully. "For the prize money. My family is kin to the Fifth House, but my father lost his fortune during the time of . . ."

"The Great Betrayal," Sola said in a low voice.

"We call it the Time of Triumph here," her husband growled. "By *his* orders."

"You mean the Shifter," Ari said casually.

Sola pressed the key to her room into Ari's hand. "May the Dreamspeaker go with you!" she whispered.

"Sola!" her husband said. "Do not speak that blessed name aloud! It is against the law!"

Ari said nothing. This then was the daily effect of the Shifter's cruel rule! Fear, fear, and more fear!

Ari left Lori and Lincoln in the rented room. The collie had been through too many adventures; he needed to rest. And Lori said bluntly that being on the *Dawnwalker* was great, except that it had made her sick to her stomach, and she was going to lie down and take a nice long nap.

Chase wanted to see the race course before they rode it. Ari took him out to the field behind the Inn. They looked at the field with horror in their hearts. The Shifter's army had set fire to the coal pits. Those pits now burned slowly. Black smoke drifted in the hot air. Dull orange flames flared in dug-out pockets of earth. The jumps for the race had been set up so that the riders would have to leap over the fiery pits.

67

"It's like the Fiery Field," Ari whispered to Chase. "It's as if the Shifter spreads his horrible land wherever he goes." Black banners drooped in the breezeless air, announcing the race would begin early in the morning. The prize was a silver rose.

Ari got on Chase's back and they walked the course. It was as difficult as she thought it would be. They drew up in front of a double oxer — a huge two-fence jump with a spread of more than seven feet over a shallow lake of low fire. Ari paced the approach, counting the number of strides Chase would have to take before he leaped it.

"That's a tough one," someone said. "But I think Cinna can take it." Ari turned and stared. The voice belonged to a boy about her own age — maybe a year older. He was tall and skinny, with bright red hair that stuck up on his head like a rooster's. He was riding a dun-colored unicorn with a pretty head and an amber horn. Cinna, the boy had called her. She nodded hello to Ari, and then flirted a little with Chase, dancing sideways and nickering in a very feminine way.

Chase rumbled back at her, then turned his attention to the boy on her back. "And who are you?"

"I'm Finn," he said cheerfully. "My parents run the Inn."

"Are you racing tomorrow?" Ari asked politely. She wished he would go away; she had too much on her mind.

"My mother won't let me," he admitted. "She thinks all the Shifter's races are fixed. She says people get hurt." He shifted in his saddle.

He looked like a decent rider — except he slouched. Ari resisted the temptation to tell him to sit up straight. She didn't know why Cinna hadn't mentioned it already. "Maybe your mother's right," Ari said, and turned back to the jump.

"You're going to ride him?" Finn jumped off Cinna and walked up to Chase. "He's amazing. My mother says he used to be a Royal unicorn. I suppose that accounts for the coat."

"Hmm?"

"How it shines. And look at his horn. It's fantastic."

"We're pretty busy right now," Ari said. "If you'll excuse us?"

"That's okay," Finn said. "I'll be quiet." He kept staring at Chase, which made Ari nervous. She knew that the Shifter would spot Chase anywhere — no matter how she disguised him — but she didn't think it'd be a good idea if the townspeople of Deridia knew much about him. "We'd prefer to be alone."

But Finn seemed impervious to snubs. "I'll hang around here for a bit." He squinted at Chase. "That's the most incredible unicorn I've ever seen."

Chase bowed. Ari recognized the ironic look in his eyes. He didn't much care for comments on his appearance. "Thank you," Ari said. She tried to

69

laugh, which sounded fake, even to her. But she had to keep it light. "You should see his sire and dam. My parents told me they were both members of the Royal stable in Balinor. Do you know what a Royal unicorn looks like?"

"There are thousands of things in the universe that I don't know about. This could be one of them. And then again maybe it isn't. But I believe you."

An honest, nosy person who didn't jump to conclusions. She would have liked Finn a lot if she weren't so worried about a shape-shifting monster and his shadow army coming after her in the race tomorrow.

Suddenly, she was overwhelmed by fear. How could she do it?! Chase, sensing her distress, rested his muzzle on her shoulder and breathed lightly into her hair.

All will be well, milady, he thought at her.

She bit her lip, not wanting to cry in front of a stranger. *Is this ever going to stop, Chase? Are we ever going to get home?* she thought back.

"Course looks pretty tough, doesn't it?" Finn said. "But if anyone can do it, I'll bet your unicorn can."

"I hope so," Ari murmured. "What if we fail?"

"There are three possibilities," the Scepter said. "One —"

"Hey!" Ari clapped her hand over the carved unicorn head, which mercifully fell silent.

"What's that?" Finn asked. He tapped his heels against Cinna's sides and walked her on down the hill.

To keep him from coming closer, Ari said curtly, "You'll never make a good rider if you don't sit up straight. You're sitting on that unicorn like a sack of potatoes." *And if your feelings are hurt,* Ari thought to herself, *maybe you'll just go away.*

Far from being insulted, Finn straightened up in the saddle, automatically balancing his weight more evenly across poor Cinna's back. Ari could have sworn a look of relief passed over the unicorn's face.

"I know I'm not a very good rider," Finn said. "Anything else I should know about good riding? I really want to learn. I need a good teacher. But to do that, I'd have to leave here. Nobody from outside Deridia ever visits here. Not since the Shifter took over. Everyone's afraid to stay here for long."

"You're actually not bad." Ari smiled at him. He was the kind of person you had to smile at eventually, since he never seemed to get mad and he wasn't insulted. "I thought that everyone accepted the Shifter's rule."

His cheerful, open face darkened a little. "I don't," he said quietly. "My parents have to, but not me. One of these days . . ."

"There are some things best left unsaid." Chase's eyes were stern. "Words like those can put my mistress in danger, Finn."

71

Chase was right. Ari bit her lip. She shouldn't be standing here with this boy. She didn't have time. "Chase and I'd better get back to the Inn," she said. "The sun's almost set."

Finn picked up his reins. "I'll race you back!"

Ari glanced up at Chase. He nodded. Adroitly, Ari leaped on his back. She tapped her heels into his sides, and with a rush, they were off.

The fields swept past them. Finn was a good rider, but he wasn't the best, by far. Ari thought his parents were right. He would get hurt if he rode in the race tomorrow. And Cinna was out of shape. She was exhausted after the first three fences.

Chase took the lead easily from Cinna, hooves pounding. His mane was like a banner. He took the fences like a low-flying bird. Ari bent over his neck, feeling the wind in her hair, the pull of his long muscles across his back. She hoped the whole competition would be like Finn and Cinna!

We can do this, Chase. We will meet the trial by fire. Together! Ari thought-spoke to Chase.

He whinnied long and loud in answer.

They clattered into the paved courtyard at the front of the stable. The usual work was going on about them. A stable hand carried buckets of manure while another swept the cobblestone yard. A third was cleaning the watering trough. Ari slid off Chase and began to take off his saddle and bridle with nimble fingers.

Finn dismounted and fiddled with the girth

to Cinna's saddle. "My mother said you're from Sixton. I've never been there. Is it . . ." His eyes traveled wistfully around the yard — at the silent workers and the depressed-looking unicorns. "Is it as busy and interesting as they say?"

"Why, yes. I suppose it is."

"They say you're a member of one of the Great Houses. Have you ever been to Balinor?"

Having to lie made Ari cross. Worry about whether the Scepter would start talking again if she inadvertently asked a question made her tense. Suddenly, she felt as if she'd been run over by a whole herd of black unicorns from the Valley of Fear.

"No, I've never been to Balinor." She shook her head and walked Chase into the stable. Behind her, Finn stood on one foot, then the other. Realizing that she wasn't going to talk to him anymore, he turned and walked away, Cinna following him.

Ari put Chase in his stall and rubbed him down with some rough sacking.

"You are sad, milady." His tone was kind.

"I feel sad for Finn. Here he is, dying for adventure and freedom in a place where he can't have either. He's so desperate, he's going to try and take that poor plump unicorn Cinna into the race tomorrow."

"She won't go far," Chase said reassuringly. "She'll have enough sense to turn around and come back to the stable if she can't handle the course. But Finn's dull life isn't what's bothering you, is it?"

"I can't make friends, Chase. I can't even talk to a boy like Finn. Not until all this is over. And yes, that makes me sad. And you? Are you doing okay?" she asked him. She ran the mane and tail comb through his silky forelock.

His dark eyes were strange and distant. "I, too, feel the burden of our quest."

She went out to get his oats from the bin near the door, then sat down in the corner of his stall and watched him eat. She sat for a long time, until the stable was dark and all the people were gone. She didn't want to return to the Inn. She didn't want to talk to anyone. She had to focus. Concentrate. There was too much that she didn't know about what lay ahead tomorrow.

But there was a way to find out.

She pulled the Royal Scepter from her belt and spoke to the unicorn head. "What will the trial by fire be like?"

The rosewood took on a warm glow. The lapis-blue eyes sparked to life.

Milady! Chase's voice was a loud alarm in her head. She jumped up, the Scepter in one hand.

"What is . . . ?" The sawdust on the floor of the stall began to roll, as if some huge form beneath it were trying to escape. Chase reared, trumpeting a battle cry. His head narrowly missed the beamed ceiling. He plunged down, his hooves raking the wooden walls. Ari leaped to his side, her booted foot coming down on top of the strange bulge.

74

The stall floor exploded! The Snakewoman's head thrust through the sand and sawdust, red forked tongue flickering, green flames coming from her fanged mouth. Ari grabbed her father's knife from her boot and swung at the head, drawing yellow-green blood from the snake's jaws.

Stand aside! Chase roared. He lowered his head, ready to spear the evil Kylie.

Ari swung the knife desperately, hitting the snaky coils again and again, until with a final violent hiss, the Snakewoman sank back and disappeared.

Ari leaned against the wall to catch her breath, her heart thudding. "And I thought we were safe from the Shifter's attacks until the race!"

It is the Scepter, milady! The power of the Scepter draws the Shifter's shadows. We cannot risk using any magic of any kind, unless we are prepared to fight!

Ari closed her eyes in despair. Chase had to be right. And Ari couldn't take the chance of a fight. Not now. Not until she won the race.

If she won the race.

And now, after this attack, she'd have to be prepared to fight whatever came after her and Chase. She thought hard for a moment, then made a couple of decisions. "Chase, I'm going to spend the night in your stall."

It was comfortable, and the straw was fresh. She filled his water bucket and groomed him again, mostly because it soothed them both. She tucked the bundle with his saddle, bridle, and saddle blanket into a corner, then settled down next to him in the straw.

Ari spent a hard night in Chase's stall. Her dreams were troubled by visions of a bloodshot Eye, searching the darkness for her and Chase. She woke once, in the dark of the night. The moon was down, the stars dim.

"Atalanta!" she cried out. "Dreamspeaker! Where are you? Why don't you speak to us?"

But she knew why. Nothing would ever be right again in Balinor unless she won this race. It was a long time before she fell asleep again.

Ari tended to Chase before the sun was up. She had no idea what kind of competition would be sent against them. They had a chance to win, she and Chase. Better than a chance. Among his own kind in Balinor, Chase was the leader of all, the best at war games, the most powerful runner. A steeplechase of three miles, no matter how rough the country or how high the jumps, should be well within his power to win.

Even though fire would bar the way.

9

Ari went back to her room after the sun was up. Lori and Linc greeted her in subdued voices. They, too, had spent a restless night.

"I hate this place," Lori muttered. "Everyone's so angry. So jumpy. It's getting on my nerves. It's creepy." Lori scowled, but then she shifted her weight and looked up at Ari. "Hey, Ari?"

"Yes, Lori."

"Good luck. I really mean it. I saw that course. It's awful."

Ari smiled, but didn't answer. She ate a hasty breakfast, then changed into her breeches and boots, keeping her soft blouse and leather vest. She wound her long bronze hair into a knot on the top of her head and looked at herself in a small warped mirror hanging near the fireplace. Her blue eyes stared back at her. There were shadows under them.

But she didn't look as scared as she felt. And that was a mercy.

She went back to the stable. She had to get ready. She had to focus. She was soaping the light, flat saddle when Finn walked into the stable, his red hair sticking up as if it had never been combed. Ari looked up from her task and greeted him with a nod. He crouched down beside her and took up the racing bridle. Like the saddle, it was made of exceptionally fine leather. It was red, traced with gold.

"That's not much of a bit for a race like this," he said. He fingered the straight iron bar.

"Chase doesn't need a heavy bit. His mouth is as light as a feather."

Finn took a sponge and the leather soap and began to clean the reins. "I found out everyone's talking about the race. The whole town will be there."

Ari didn't say anything. She walked Chase into the open air. Finn followed her, carrying the saddle and bridle. The paved yard was filled with riders in breeches and riding boots. The unicorns talked among themselves. Chase lifted his head and occasionally whinnied back.

"You doing okay, Chase?" Ari asked.

"Yes," he said briefly.

"Chase doesn't talk much?" Finn began to clean the bit again with strong swipes of the tack cloth.

"When he has something to say." Ari rested the jump saddle on her knees and looked at him.

"No offense, Finn, but I'm really busy here. Can't you find a spot to watch the race?"

His eyes were a deep, liquid brown. When he squinted, as he did now, his long eyelashes almost hid them. "I'm going to ride along."

Ari stared at him, openmouthed. Then she said, "You're kidding. You're good, Finn, but you're not that good. I mean, these are pretty tough jumps." Almost immediately, she was sorry she'd been so blunt. But she didn't want to have to worry about Finn while she was trying to win this race. And she wasn't at all sure if the "fire" part of this trial would be limited to the burning pits. Would the woods themselves burst into flame? Would ghouls from the Valley of Fear jump out from concealed spots, waving flaming torches? No, she didn't want to worry about the safety of a novice rider in the coming thirty minutes.

"I'm going to walk through," he said calmly.

"Will the judges allow that?" Any unicorn and rider could "walk through," that is, go through the gates rather than over fences, if the judges allowed it. But riders that walked through did it because they wanted to enjoy the ride. And this course, with its pits of fire, was going to be terrible.

"My father asked. It'll be okay, as long as I don't get in anybody's way."

"I'd appreciate it if you'd keep out of *our* way," she said as nicely as possible. "It's pretty important that I win this race."

79

"I thought maybe it was." His freckled face was serious.

Ari looked sharply at him. How much had he seen and heard yesterday? He was such a quiet kind of person; she might not even have noticed him. Had he overheard her conversations with Chase? Had he really left the stable when she thought he had? Could he have seen Kylie burst through the floor of Chase's stall?

Chase had been standing quietly while Ari started to fit the red silk pad over his withers. Suddenly, he stiffened as if he'd been struck with a whip. His head came up. A hot, fiery anger flamed in his eyes, then disappeared so fast that Ari wasn't sure she had seen it.

The sun darkened, as if a shadow had passed over it. She whirled. A rider stood in the open door to the stable, leading a coal-black unicorn. It was a huge stallion, powerfully built, with a heavy, brutal muzzle and flat black eyes. The horn in the middle of his forehead had been sharpened to a killing point.

She knew that unicorn! Moloth!

The rider was dressed from head to foot in black: black breeches, black shirt, and a black gauze mask that was pulled down over his head. The eyeless mask stared in her direction. The black unicorn drew his lips back from his teeth in a grotesque grin.

Moloth! Chase shouted wordlessly. He sprang forward. Ari yelled, "Halt!" and made a grab for his mane. Chase came to a quivering halt. The rider lifted his riding crop in a quick, insolent salute. He reached inside his jacket with one gloved hand and dropped a red rose onto the floor. The thorns were long and pointed. The heart of the rose was filled with cankers and black spots.

Fearfully, Ari picked it up.

The shadow lifted from the light. Ari blinked. Both the unicorn and the rider were gone.

"Who was that?" Finn said. A frown crossed his face. He put a watchful hand on Ari's arm. She shook it off impatiently.

"Chase?" she said, careful to keep her voice neutral and unalarmed. "Was that who it seemed to be?"

"Moloth," the unicorn head said from inside her leather vest. "Herd leader of the shadow unicorns and favored mount of Entia himself."

Entia's unicorn! Ari's bones turned to water. That featureless face! That thin-lipped grin. Would she ride against Entia himself? She was afraid to voice the thought. Afraid to hear the Scepter's response. Dizzy with fear, she slumped to the ground.

"Here, put your head between your knees," Finn said. His hand was strong and gentle on the back of her neck. "Do you know that rider?"

Moloth! Chase growled in her mind. *And on his back — a human I do not know!*

Is it the Shifter, Chase?

Finally, he shook his head, his bridle jingling. *A stranger, milady. Not the Shifter himself, but one of his own.*

Ari pulled herself together. She smiled at Finn as brightly as she could. "Didn't eat enough breakfast," she said lightly. "I'm fine now."

"Let me get you something to eat. Some fruit or something."

Just go away! Ari thought. Her nerves were strained to the breaking point. But aloud she said, "Thanks. Maybe a piece of bread."

She didn't even notice when Finn left. She finished putting the red silk pad on Chase's back, then fit the saddle in place, leaving the girth buckled but loose. She checked the length of the stirrups and made a small adjustment. She took Chase's head between her hands and gazed earnestly into his eyes. "Hang on, Chase! Just a little longer. Give me all you've got, my friend. For all our sakes."

She swung herself into the saddle and rode out into the sunlight. Mounted riders were all over the paved yard, checking their girths and stirrups, swallowing a few gulps of water, or just quietly riding in circles, preparing for the race.

Lincoln and Lori stood back from the crowd

of onlookers. Lori raised her hand in a brief salute. Ari looked around the paved yard, afraid to see the Shadow Rider — and afraid not to see him. None of the other unicorns were black stallions, and all of the riders were dressed in regular breeches and soft jerkins and vests. If she'd been less ruthlessly honest with herself, Ari would have thought she'd imagined that malignant smile and the cocky salute.

But she knew Moloth and his sinister rider were nearby.

Lori came up to her and put a worried hand on her stirrup. "Everything seems normal for a race," she said in an undertone. "Just do the best you can." She smiled. "You're the best rider here, Ari. And you have the best mount."

"We're cheering for you!" Lincoln said. His tone was brave, but his eyes were worried.

"I'm betting on her and Chase to win," Finn said, coming up behind her. Ari jumped in the saddle. Chase shifted restlessly under her. That boy had a genius for appearing out of nowhere! "I brought you bread and juice."

Ari accepted the food with the best grace she could muster. The bread was like ashes in her mouth, and the juice tasted sour. "I thought you were going to ride through, Finn. Is Cinna ready?"

"Cinna's pulled up lame. There's another unicorn I can ride, though. I'll be there!" He put his hands on her stirrup and stared earnestly into her face. "There's a reason why I have to be there, Ari. This is my chance to do something big. To get out of Deridia!"

"I don't understand."

"I had this dream last night, Ari. A wonderful —"

A horn sounded. Ari straightened up with an exclamation. The riders began to gather at the first gate. With a last look at her, Finn took off running toward the barn.

Ari tapped Chase's side lightly with both heels and moved into position. The sun shone steadily, illuminating every corner of the yard. No Shadow Rider lurked there. All of the competitors moved out to the course at a slow walk. They lined up at the edge of the field, side by side. The judge shouted instructions that Ari barely heard. She tightened her girth, checked her stirrup leathers for the fifth time, and gathered the reins in both hands.

"On your mark!" the judge shouted.

The riders tensed. Quiet descended.

"Get set!"

Ari put her heels down and rose a little in the saddle. The first jump was about twenty paces away. It was an easy one. No fire beneath it or around it. Just the field and a three-rail fence.

"And . . . GO!"

The horn sounded. The flag dropped. Chase sprang forward with a powerful thrust of his hind legs. Ari felt a surge of excitement as the two of them took the lead immediately. She turned her head to glance at the rest of the field. . . .

He was there. Moloth and the Shadow Rider. Galloping easily at Chase's heels, a glint of red fire behind the gauze mask.

Ari clenched her teeth. The race was on.

10

Ari bent low over Chase's neck, the grit-filled wind stinging her cheeks. She held her hands low and kept her head down. Chase surged beneath her, his flying hooves sending up patches of dirt and grass.

Moloth and the Shadow Rider galloped beside them. The blank, featureless shield over the rider's face reflected the sun.

The second fence loomed ahead. Ari sent an urgent thought to Chase: *Five feet high! Maybe more! And there's a pit of fire beneath it.*

Chase responded by shifting his weight off his forehand and gathering in his powerful hindquarters. He cleared the jump easily.

The two unicorns, one coal-black and one glorious bronze, had left the rest of the field behind. They raced side by side. The Shadow Rider leaned to the side. Ari caught a glimpse of a swinging mace. The chain glinted brutally in the sunlight.

Ride on! she shouted to Chase. She dug her heels into his sides, and he gave her a burst of speed.

The mace swung high and down, whistling past Ari's ear.

Missed!

The next fence came up fast. Too fast. The flames beneath the pit licked high around the end posts. Ari was late with the cue to shift Chase's weight off his forehand and onto his hindquarters. He took the fence late, stumbling just before he lifted off. Ari slipped off the saddle and clung to her unicorn's side. She closed her eyes as he leaped, clinging with both hands to his mane, her right foot out of the stirrup and hooked into the cantle. Hot fire seared her back as they arched over the fence. She used the force of Chase's landing to swing herself back into the saddle.

The Shadow Rider and Moloth took the fence easily. The rider raised his right hand —

And a stream of fire shot out from his glove!

Chase jumped sideways in midstride. Another flame shot past Chase, singeing the hair on his flanks. Ari was jolted out of the saddle and fell onto Chase's neck.

Easy, Chase! She caught her breath, and sobbed. She righted herself once again, kicking the stirrups into place under her boots, settling deep into the saddle. "Go! Go! Go!" she said into his ear. "Ride on, Chase! Ride on!"

He answered her with speed. His head came up and he ran as he had never run before. The Shadow Rider fell behind. Chase took the third fence, then the fourth. The dry and dusty field flashed by.

The course took a sharp right turn here. Ari flexed with her left rein and drew in her right. She pressed her right leg behind the girth, and Chase curved in a perfect turn.

The fifth fence. The sixth. Moloth thundered along behind them. Flames shot from his muzzle. Ari felt the fiery breath on her neck. She swallowed her fear. The seventh fence. The eight and ninth. Sweat from Chase's chest flew into her eyes. The Shadow Rider screamed a wordless wail of anger and hate. The terrible cry unleashed a torrent of fire from the pit beneath the next jump, and Ari rode through a wall of green-yellow flames so hot and high she could barely see the course ahead.

And still Chase kept ahead of the Shadow Rider!

The tenth fence was an oxer, a tricky double-width jump of logs and brush. Chase saw it, wavered, and Ari balanced herself on his back, murmuring words of love and encouragement through the wall of fire.

He made it!

The next jump was over water. Behind them, the Shadow Rider flung flame after flame from his mailed fist. Chase's breath was coming in deep gasps. Ari sat back in the saddle and raced him through the water jump, not over, giving him a short respite from the brutal leaps, hoping the stream would halt the flames, at least for a moment.

She was right. The fire died down as the Shadow Rider and Moloth followed her through the water. Chase scrambled out of the stream and up the bank. She slammed her left leg against Chase's side, and he swerved into the woods. Ari flexed him down to a canter, squeezing left, right, left, right as they worked their way through the trees. She pulled him to a halt behind a large, broad-leaved oak tree.

She heard the crash of branches and the crackle of flames as the Shadow Rider entered the woods. The black unicorn was breathing deeply, his harsh breaths punctuated by the sound of trampled brush. She stroked Chase's neck, her hand trembling.

A ball of fire rolled toward her. She ducked without thinking.

"Ari!" A hissing whispered in the woods. Ari gripped the reins.

"Ari! This way!" A giant red unicorn emerged from the trees near the oak. Ari was so astonished, she didn't recognize the rider at first. Then she saw the red hair sticking up and a flash of freckles on a bit of wrist exposed between glove and shirt.

"Finn!"

"Follow me! My unicorn knows the way out! There's a cave!"

Rednal! Chase said in her mind. The great bronze unicorn moved eagerly beneath her. *Rednal!*

The red stallion whickered in response.

"Oh, Chase!" Ari blurted. "Chase! Who is that? Can we trust him?"

The Royal Scepter tied to her waist came to life again at Ari's question. "His Majesty's brother, Rednal of the rainbow herd."

"But, why?" Ari kept her voice low. She looked nervously over her shoulder. A spear of flame flared in the woods, perhaps three hundred yards away.

"Rednal has been sent by Atalanta to guide you to victory," the unicorn head said.

"But, Finn! Why is Finn riding him?"

"We don't have much time," Finn interrupted urgently. "You have to complete the course, Ari. I'll meet you at the cave!"

The flames coursed into the sky at her left. The Shadow Rider had discovered them! With a great crash of branches, Moloth burst through the trees. Finn shouted, waved, and took off like a shot. The Shadow Rider didn't hesitate. He couldn't see Ari and Chase behind the tree. All he saw was a great red unicorn. He smacked the huge black unicorn on the neck with a mailed fist. Moloth leaped forward, and they ran after Finn and Rednal.

Ari waited until the sounds of galloping hooves faded into the distance. Then she rode Chase out from the safety of the sheltering tree. She sat for a moment, getting her bearings.

The Shadow Rider had mistaken Rednal for Chase. But the illusion wouldn't hold up if the Shadow Rider got too close. That meant there was very little time to complete the course and get to the safety of the cave.

If the cave were safe! What if this were a trick of the Shifter!

Ari pushed aside the fear that Finn's appearance was a trick or a hoax. She had to trust someone. And if her trust were misplaced . . . she would just have to figure out what to do when that happened.

But right now she had to complete the course. She had to win the silver rose.

She rode Chase back to the stream. The last of the field of riders was just coming through it. She joined them as unobtrusively as possible, hoping to gain the head of the field again at the eighteenth jump.

The final jump on the steeplechase course was a huge briar hedge. There were no pits of fire, just thick branches armed with wicked-looking thorns. Ari crouched over Chase's neck and urged him on. He gave her one last, mighty effort, surging ahead of the field of riders. Three strides short of the hedge, she rose in the saddle, and he moved off his forehand, ready to jump.

Flame snaked across Ari's back. She screamed and lost the reins. Moloth and the Shadow Rider seemed to rise out of nowhere. In the fire and the confusion, Ari dimly heard Finn shout, "The cave! Head for the cave!" Rednal's whinny cut over the roaring flames and Chase twitched his ears back . . . then leaped . . . and somehow they were over the briar.

Villagers were gathered at the end of the race. A ragged cheer rose from the crowd.

They had won!

Chase was galloping too fast! His forelegs gave way and he fell. Ari bounced free and rolled. She scrambled to her feet. Behind the briar hedge, the Shadow Rider shook his fist and raved word-lessly at them. They had won! They had won! It didn't matter if the Shadow Rider followed them now — they had won!

Finn and Rednal leaped the hedge and landed near Chase. Ari ran to Chase and grabbed the reins trailing in the grass. He lay on his side, grunting with pain. She knelt next to him. She fum-bled for the leather bag Dr. Bohnes had given her. Surely Chase wasn't badly hurt! Surely the first magic could help him!

Her hands were slick with sweat. She heard the beat of hooves; the rest of the field was coming.

She pulled Chase to his feet with encouraging clucks of her tongue.

"Hurry!" Finn cried. "You have to follow me! We have to get out of here!"

"But we've won!" Ari cried.

"It doesn't matter! I mean — it does, but the Shifter can still try and kidnap you! We've got to get out of Deridia!"

On the other side of the fence, the Shadow Rider swung easily off Moloth, and drew out an iron spear that had been hanging from his belt. Behind them all, the field of riders came across the meadow, headed for the final fence.

Chase got to his feet with a groan. His left foreleg was swollen. Ari dipped her hand into Dr. Bohnes's bag and pulled out a small vial of salve.

"Hurry!" Finn cried.

"We must go!" Rednal shouted.

The crowd of villagers stirred. A short, burly man in the front started to walk toward them. His face was scowling.

Ari's heart pounded. She rubbed the salve on Chase's leg. Almost instantly, the swelling began to die down.

The villagers surged forward, following the burly man. "Hey!" he shouted. "You weren't supposed to win!"

"H-o-o-o-ld them!" The Shadow Rider's voice was like hollow thunder. "Hold them, if you value your li-ives!"

The Rider's voice inflamed Chase. The mighty unicorn stood tall. His ebony horn flashed with light. His deep eyes were angry. His coat glowed with the sheen of hammered metal. His hooves gleamed bright black. His mane and tail flowed wild and free.

"MOLOTH!" he shouted.

Ari threw her arms around his neck. From the other side of the fence, she heard Moloth's guttural response:

"SUNCHASER!"

Chase reared and wheeled. His muscled forelegs pawed the sky. He addressed his ancient enemy: "Moloth! I will come for you!"

"Chase!" Ari said. "CHASE! We can't stop to fight now!"

The Shadow Rider remounted, and in one fluid motion he and the shadow unicorn were over the fence. Moloth faced Chase and reared, flames streaming from his nose. His eyes were a maddened red.

A heavyset gray unicorn was now in the lead of the steeplechase field. As Moloth and Chase began lunging at each other, ready to fight, the gray flinched on his way over the briar hedge. He fell into Moloth as he landed, and the two unicorns tumbled together in a confusion of horns and hooves. The gray's rider tumbled to the ground and got up limping. The unicorns and riders behind the gray crashed into one another in a yelling heap.

"Come on!" Finn yelled. "The cave!" He swung himself into Rednal's saddle. Ari scrambled up Chase's side, and without pausing to fit her feet in the stirrups, they raced for their lives.

Slipping, sliding, they crashed through the trees. Finn guided them toward a cliff rising from the forest floor. Moloth's angry screams pushed them on. The shadow unicorn had regained his feet! The Shadow Rider was after them again!

"There!" Finn shouted, pointing at the cliff. "It's there! A way out of Deridia!"

Ari stared. A huge wooden door was set into the side of the cliff.

"The Scepter, milady!" Chase shouted.

She pulled the Scepter out and held it up. With a groan and a creak, the door swung open. "We won the race!" she shouted, her voice clear and confident. "We passed the trial by fire!" Darkness gaped beyond the open door. Ari rode Chase straight into it. Finn and Rednal crowded behind her. With a mighty clang the wooden door swung shut, right in the Shadow Rider's face.

Chase charged forward. His hooves slipped on the stones.

They fell forward into a deeper black than she had ever seen before.

11

"Now this," Finn shouted with joy, "is a lot better than Deridia!"

Ari blinked, rubbed her eyes, and sat up. There was sand in her hair. The sound of waves and seagulls bewildered her. The sun was high in the blue sky.

Where were they?

She got to her feet, spilling sand from her boots, her shirt, and her hair. A long white beach curved into the distance. Sapphire water sparkled in the sunlight. Finn rode Rednal bareback along the sand, his red hair sticking straight up. Chase swam strongly in the surf, his ebony horn held high against the white caps. He turned and saw Ari standing up, then he thundered out of the ocean, blue water cascading down his bronze coat.

"You slept so long, milady!" He bent his head and breathed into her hair. Ari, blinking back tears, threw her arms around his neck and hugged him until she had no hugs left.

"What happened, Chase? How did we get here?" She laughed for joy and looked around. "And where *is* here?"

"We don't know," Chase said. "But we have overcome the first challenge! The trial by fire is over!"

Ari looked at him. For a moment, no words passed between them. Then Chase said, "We fell through that tunnel for a long time. You passed out on my back. I think you may have hit your head as we fell. We landed here in a place of fresh water and bright sun. Finn found Dr. Bohnes's bag and rubbed your temples with the salve that healed my leg. Then you fell into a deep natural sleep." He nodded toward the perimeter where the beach ended and a wildflower meadow began. "There is a clear stream there. I will take you to drink."

"It's beautiful here!" Ari rubbed her head. She could feel a welt on her forehead. "But where *is* here?"

"You will discover that in time," the Scepter said from between the folds of her skirt.

Ari drew it aloft. The blue light was as faint as it had been in Deridia. Ari had a feeling that this dimming of the light was the result of the balance of magic still being out of whack. "Is it . . . is this the second challenge?"

"Maybe. Maybe not," the Scepter said in an

infuriating way. "All I want to say is that none of this would be happening if you hadn't taken me out of Balinor."

"But I didn't know this would happen!"

"That's true," Chase said. "We didn't know. But it doesn't change anything." He nudged Ari with his muzzle. "I do not know why we are here, milady. We shall see what the Deep Magic sends us."

"But Lori and Lincoln? They're still back in Deridia! Are they all right? And what about Captain Tredwell?"

"Trust in the Deep Magic," the Scepter said crossly. "Don't worry about them, Your Royal Highness. They wait for you on the ship. You will rejoin them if . . ." The Scepter scowled. "Never mind. I'm going back to sleep. Wake me up when you've finished the job. If you finish the job."

"We don't have much of a choice, milady. We must wait on events." Chase knelt beside her so that she could climb on his back without stress. She swung her leg over his back, and tried to relax as Chase got to his feet. He was right. All they could do was wait.

Chase trotted briskly to the verge of the beach, then made his way down a short path that led to a clear bubbling spring. Ari slipped off and drank her fill.

She sat by the brook with a happy sigh. This place was beautiful in a way she had never experienced before. Huge tropical flowers bloomed in glossy green bushes. Palm trees lifted crowned heads to the sky. Brightly colored birds darted among the trees, their sweet trills recalling the tones of Atalanta's lovely voice. The burdens of being a princess seemed far away.

Ari leaned back on her elbows, relishing the peace. Chase stood beside her, idly switching his tail. He raised his head, and gently lifted a ripe fruit from the tree above them, using his horn. It fell and rolled to Ari's feet. She picked it up and bit into the juicy flesh. It was so sweet and cooling that she felt she'd never be thirsty again. "I do believe that Rednal and Finn saved our lives," she said after a long moment. "Why do you suppose Atalanta chose him to ride Rednal?"

"I do not know. He is a brave young man. And he hates the Shifter." Then Chase added thoughtfully, "Rednal says that he rides well. You might consider giving him a place in the Royal Cavalry when we regain the throne."

"There's still the next challenge to meet," Ari said. "The ordeal by moonlight!" She leaped to her feet, the memory of the challenges an unpleasant cloud on her mood. "I'll race you to the beach!"

Chase won — of course! He raced ahead of her and then rolled in the sand as if he were a colt again.

Ari pulled off her boots and took off her vest.

She wriggled her toes in the white sand. Dressed only in breeches and a blouse, she plunged into the turquoise waves with Rednal and Finn.

At the end of that wonderful day, the sun dropped beyond the blue horizon as suddenly as a hunting falcon. A blue twilight reigned for only a short while, and then the moon came up. Huge and golden, it was swollen with light like one of the tropical fruits they had munched during the day.

Rednal and Chase cropped the short grass at the edge of the beach and drank from the brook. Finn, who announced that he was tired of fruit, fashioned a net from the dried fronds of a palm tree, and emerged triumphant from the sea with two fat fish. Then, to Ari's amazement, he produced a box of waterproof matches from his pocket and built a small fire.

They roasted the fish over the flames. It tasted wonderful, that fish. At the end of the meal, Finn scooted up a palm tree and brought down a coconut.

"That will be delicious, but it'll be hard to open," she said. "Anyway, I'm really full." She relaxed with a happy sigh and looked over at Finn. "I want to thank you for helping Chase and me win the first trial," she said. "But why did you do it?"

Finn poked at the fire with his toe. The tips of his ears were red. "I hated what happened to Deridia. After the Shifter took over, everything changed." He wrinkled his nose in disgust. "I didn't think that I could do anything about it. I mean, my parents depend on the villagers to come to the Inn and keep the business open. We hate the Shifter — all three of us. But what could we do? What could I do against him and his men? And the shadow unicorns . . ." He shuddered, and tossed another branch onto the fire. "Anyway. Last night, after I met you" — the tips of his ears turned a brighter pink — "I had this dream." He raised his eyes. His face was filled with wonder. "The most beautiful unicorn came to me. She had the saddest violet eyes. She said you needed a champion. And that she would send someone to help me be your champion." He gave Rednal an amused look. "So when Big Red here showed up, I was ready."

"I'm glad you were," Ari said softly.

Finn shrugged his shoulders and rolled the coconut over in the sand.

"You'll never get that open, Finn," Chase said with a mischievous look in his eye. He bent down on his forelegs and neatly opened up the hard shell with a slash of his ebony horn.

The inside of the fruit was black! A horrible odor arose from the two halves. Finn made a disgusted face. Ari, her heart hammering, knew what that awful smell meant.

This was the Shifter's work. She waited a long moment before she picked up the halves. She picked up the piece of paper folded inside and read:

CATCH THE ROSE!
MOONLIGHT DIVING COMPETITION!
ALL COMPETITORS WELCOME!

And at the bottom of the note, a white rose was inscribed. Its petals were deformed and insects crawled at its heart. The rose itself was twisted around a malignant shape: a monstrous squid. Its beak gaped wide. A single dark red eye glowed at her.

"What is it, Ari?" Finn asked.

"Nothing," she said hastily. She folded the note and tucked it into her breeches pocket.

Milady? Chase's tones were concerned.

"Not now, Chase," she said aloud. Her heart sank. Her hands were cold, despite the warmth of the fire. There was no time, no date on the announcement of the second challenge.

Ari leaned back on her elbows beside the dying fire. Maybe she had a little more time. A day, perhaps? Maybe two? Chase was exhausted from the violence of the steeplechase. She was, too. If she had just a little more time to relax, to get to know Finn better. She wanted to tell him who she really was. She knew, somehow, that she could trust the red-haired boy. And she needed friends on this terrifying journey to win her homeland back!

She closed her eyes, safe under the watchful gaze of Chase, Rednal, and Finn. Strange to think that fire could be so cozy here — and so terrifying in the claws of the Shifter!

"What's the matter?" Finn asked abruptly. "You look sad."

"Nothing." Ari rubbed her hands over her face. In the friendly shadows beyond the fire, Chase was asleep on his feet. Rednal snoozed beside him. A nightbird chirped happily in the rustling treetops. "I just wish . . . I wish . . ."

"That you didn't have to go back to your home in Sixton?"

Ari looked straight at him. She couldn't tell him the truth. Not yet. "How did you know that?"

"I feel just like you must feel," he said simply. "I know that you are nobly born, but you said that your family lost its fortune."

"In a way," Ari said cautiously.

"So you have to depend on someone else for food to feed you and your unicorn, for the clothes on your back, for the boots on your feet. And because you depend on them, they control you. You don't have any freedom. Well, I have freedom now. And so do you, Ari! It's great! We can do anything we want! We can ride Rednal and Chase anywhere! We can both be free!"

Ari shook her head. "I can't, Finn. I have a job to do. The race through fire? It's not the only challenge I have to pass. There's something waiting here, too. An ordeal by moonlight."

"I can help!"

"I don't think you can. Not this time." She fought back tears. "It's too hard, this job I have to do," she admitted in a low voice. "I wish we could stay here forever."

Finn gave her a sympathetic look. He blushed a little. "I know that you're not an ordinary person. For one thing — you can use magic."

"Some," Ari said, a little hesitantly.

"So whoever you are, Ari-from-Sixton, we're bound to have some pretty interesting adventures. And that's all I want from life right now. A chance. Just a chance to do something different."

Ari brought her knees up to her chin and stared thoughtfully into the fire. "I will tell you all of it. Someday. Someday soon."

12

The night wore on. They all slept. Ari woke from a dream of Atalanta. The Dreamspeaker was standing in front of a pair of scales. The Scales of Magic. The scales were almost balanced, but not quite.

It was time for the second challenge.

Ari was seized by a powerful urge to walk the beach. She tucked the Royal Scepter near Finn's outstretched hand. If anything happened to her, Chase would see that Finn carried it to safety. She checked the knife at her belt. Barefoot, she walked along the water's edge.

The water was warm. Starlight caught the tips of the gentle waves and made them sparkle. The sand was firm beneath her feet, and she jogged a little way for the sheer joy of it. Her legs, broken and scarred from her very first trip through the Gap — when she had first been sent to Glacier River

Farm — were whole and strong again. Her face was pleasantly sunburned, and her skin had that soft relaxed feel that only comes after swimming in tropical oceans.

She wondered where this place really was. If she left, would she ever find it again?

But for now! It was so lovely! Hard to believe that the Shifter would send her a trial here, in this wonderful place.

She turned to stare out at the ocean, to impress the memory of this place forever in her mind. The heavy moonlight made a golden path on the water. It looked solid enough to walk on. The moonlight began just at the water's edge, right in front of her toes. It stretched out into the little bay formed by the beach. Ari narrowed her eyes to see. It was almost as if — no, the moonlit path *did* end at a mound of black rock. And on the rock was a figure washed around with silver. Were there mermaids here, in this wonderful place?

"Ari!" The voice was low and kind. "Ari! Walk out to see me!"

"Can I walk on the water?" Ari said.

The figure raised one arm. A ball of silver light spun from its fingers and rolled along the golden path. "Now try," the mysterious stranger said.

Ari shrugged and put one bare foot into the edge of the water. Solid warmth wrapped around her toes and under her heel. She tested her weight on the golden surface. She stood on one foot. She could feel the ocean beneath her as almost a living thing, but the surface of the path held. She put her other foot down, and arms outstretched, as if she were on a balance beam, she walked toward the black rock.

"Come closer," the voice invited.

Caution held Ari back. But the ocean was so calm, the night so beautiful, and the voice so kind — there couldn't be any danger here!

"There isn't." The silvery figure stirred on the rocks. Ari couldn't really see it — no, her — she decided. It was a woman's voice that called her.

"Ari!" Half-laughing, filled with gentle reproach, the woman stretched her arms out. "Come to me!"

A mermaid! Her silvery tail slapped the water gently. Her long silver hair fell about her shoulders to her waist. And her eyes . . .

Did she see a red glint in them? Was there a flash of the Shifter's own fiery gaze?

Ari stood still. Waves lapped on either side of the narrow path of moonlight. The whole world was ocean, the land with her friends and Chase far behind her.

The mermaid held out her hand. She held a rose. It was white. Ari could see the wilted leaves, the insects crawling around its decaying heart. So this *was* it. The second challenge.

She stepped onto the rocks. The light from the heavy gold moon flooded the mermaid sitting there. A thin circlet of flashing jewels around her white forehead bound her brow. She held out the rose, a mocking smile on her lips. Then she dropped it into the depths of the sea.

Ari clenched her fists, then took a deep breath. She dove straight as an arrow into the waves. She spiraled down into the water, her bronze hair floating behind her. Above her, she could see the heavy moon through the ceiling of ocean. Below, the rose spun down to a translucent green world. There was a quick, sinuous movement next to her in the water. Ari turned slowly, kicking her feet and holding her breath. The mermaid flashed by, arms by her sides, kicking strongly as she headed to the city beneath the waves. The knife-edge of her tail slashed at Ari's ankles, drawing blood from Ari's foot, which made a brownish cloud, spreading silently around her.

The monstrous mermaid swam toward the city. The Shifter's underwater city! Houses and roads and palaces of jagged coral were revealed by the mysterious green light! A giant squid stared up at Ari with evil red eyes. Mermaids and mermen with sword-tipped tails swam leisurely along. Dark sea horses with flat eyes drew carts along roads made of lava rock so sharp it could cut flesh to ribbons.

The white rose spun deeper and deeper.

Ari needed to breathe. She let the last of her breath go in a spume of bubbles. She had to get to the surface — had to breathe. But she would dive down again and get the rose.

She broke the surface of the water with a huge gasp and inhaled great gulps of air. The pile of rocks was no more than three yards away. She swam toward it, then pulled herself up, to catch her breath.

She clambered onto the rock and peered below. The rose swayed in the currents. Some trick of the moonlight made it seem just out of reach. One hand clinging to the rock, she slipped into the water again, groping for it.

A huge shape burst out of the water! Razor teeth snapped at her wrist. Ari drew her knife and slashed out without pausing to think. The knife drew dark blood from one of the many arms. The creature recoiled, bellowing, thrashing wildly with its tentacles.

She had encountered this monster before. It was Sistern! The horrible creature of the Shifter that guarded the Palace moat! Sistern's beak snapped at her hands. Salt water stung her eyes. The wind rose, whipping her hair into her face.

Ari slashed harder at Sistern's tentacles. She drew greenish blood, which looked almost black in the moonlight! If she could just reach the creature's eye! She thrust upward. Her knife tore into spongy flesh. Sistern's shriek froze Ari's heart and stopped her breath.

Sistern sank hissing and shrieking beneath the boiling waves. And there in the middle of the whirlpool was the rose. Ari set her teeth and plunged into the water. She swam hard against the whirling current. The water now was cold and the moonlit path from the rocks to the shore had been dissolved by whatever evil magic had summoned Sistern from the ocean's depths. The waves grew higher and the wind picked up. The monster's last wailing shriek was carried away by the steadily increasing gale.

The rose! She had to get the rose! Ari took a deep breath and plunged down, down, down. Cold currents swept through her trailing hair. She held her eyes open straining to see the white flower, lit by the yellow-green of the Shifter's underwater city and the glow of the huge moon above. Her fingertips brushed it but it swirled out of reach. She kicked harder, her breath bursting in her chest. On the far side of the coral city below, a small army of mermaids and mermen gathered. They swam in excited circles. Their leader was the silvery mermaid who had called Ari out to the rocks. With a flash of their sword-tipped tails, they began to swim toward her, their red eyes alight with fury. Ari reached. Grabbed.

The rose was hers! She clutched it and the thorns tore her hand. She swam blindly to the surface. She broke free of the water, gasping for air. Dark clouds scudded across the sky, hiding the tropical moon.

The shore seemed farther and farther away with every kick of her feet. Her legs, which had been feeling whole and healthy again, began to cramp. Ari stopped, treaded water again, and rubbed futilely at her calves. Seawater slapped into her mouth and nose. She inhaled a great gulp and choked on the bitter taste. The waves rose over her head.

She glanced backward. The merpeople rose in a body from the waves. They grinned horribly, showing pointed teeth. Ari kicked and swam, kicked and swam.

Oh, Chase, she thought miserably. *Oh, Chase.* Her arms ached with the effort of staying afloat. The rose drew blood from her tightly clenched fingers. The sudden storm was fierce, and she could no longer see the shoreline.

I won't give up, she said to herself. *I. Will. Not. Give. Up!* If she was going to breathe her last breath, it was going to be swimming toward land, not just giving up and sinking beneath the waves.

She forced her arms to move. Gave a couple of kicks with her weary legs.

"Milady?"

"Chase?"

He was there. Somehow, in the noise and torment of the storm, he had found her. He took a breath, ducked under, and she felt his back on her feet. He rose up, swimming strongly. She grabbed his mane with a cold hand. He pulled her on, his breath steady, his hide a living warmth in the cold sea.

The eerie wails of the merpeople came closer, closer.

A fishtail sliced her side. Another must have hit Chase; she felt him jerk. But he swam on, his great chest heaving, his legs churning the waves. Ari slashed backward with the knife and a scream like a dying seagull split the air. Chase's horn dipped into the waves and dipped again. Ari saw the red eyes of the silver-haired mermaid slip beneath the waves.

An eternity of wind and waves passed before Chase found the sand and they stumbled on shore. Finn was there with Rednal. Finn held a stout branch, ready to attack if the merpeople appeared from the waves. Rednal's bright horn was lowered menacingly. The wind whipped Rednal's mane around his horn and tumbled Finn's red hair into spikes.

"We didn't think you'd make it!" the boy shouted into the tumult. "Are you okay?"

Ari held on to Chase's mane and dragged herself to her feet. The soft tropical night was gone as if it had never existed. The wind whipped at her face so hard, she could barely hear him. "I made it!" she gasped. "Do you have the Scepter?"

"What?"

"I said, do you have the Scepter?"

"Yes!" Finn struggled with the bundle of clothes over his arm and disentangled the Scepter.

Ari lurched toward it and took it in both hands. "Hey!" she shouted to it. She held the rose in front of the wooden head. "HEY! That was the second challenge! The ordeal by moonlight. We won, Chase and I! NOW GET US OUT OF HERE!"

"That's telling it!" Finn shouted. He jumped up and down, raising his fist in the air.

The rosewood scepter glowed with blue light. The wooden head blinked, perhaps from the stinging sand.

"Well?" Ari demanded.

". . . question," Rednal shouted.

"What?"

"I said you have to ask it a question!"

"Oh!" Ari struggled to stand upright in the buffeting wind. There was a sudden rattle of thunder and a flash of lightning. Rain poured from the sky as if someone had opened a giant faucet. Ari brought the Scepter close to her lips and said, "Which is the way out?"

"Congratulations," the Scepter said. "You've passed the second challenge. And the way out? It's right this way."

14

The storm was so deafening; Ari wasn't sure afterward exactly how they found their way off the tropical island and back to the world of Balinor. Lightning cracked again and again, illuminating the thundering waves in violet flashes. Ari and Finn mounted the unicorns. Ari led the way, the Scepter held in front of her like a beacon. They found a wooden door, sunk horizontally into the sand. Finn struggled off Rednal and opened it. Then they descended down an endless series of winding steps. Ari grew dizzy with fatigue. She saw — or did she imagine it? — hideous monsters in the gloom of the caverns beneath the sands. Kylie's slitted yellow eyes seem to follow them and a single, red-veined Eye floated above them like a poisonous moon. The shadow unicorns also joined them, silent except for the strike of their iron hooves against the rocks.

But the Shifter's forces didn't attack — if it were they, and not mere illusion.

At the very end of the journey, the air turned cold. They stumbled out of the cavern and onto a high plateau. It was raining. The rain became snow, the snow a blizzard. The Royal Scepter glowed more brightly in the whirling white. Ari, Chase, Finn, and Rednal climbed up a mountain that never seemed to end. Ari's breath made white frosty patterns in the freezing air. Several times she slipped off Chase's back to clean the snow and ice that had balled up in his hooves. Finn did the same for Rednal.

They reached the summit of the mountain, and without pause, plunged down the other side.

The snow died away. A grudging dawn cast a dim light. Ari could see Chase's frost-rimmed face.

A familiar sun rose behind them, and Ari paused, the Scepter still aloft in one hand.

"Look, Finn! The shore of the Sixth Sea! And there — see it? That beautiful green ship with the creamy sails? That's the *Dawnwalker!*"

Finn was panting heavily. He wiped his nose with his shirtsleeve and stood beside her, looking down. "That's good news?" he asked doubtfully. "I mean, can we trust this? What if it's just more of the Shifter's work?"

"Nope," Ari said confidently. "Look. See that man at the stern? That's Captain Tredwell. He must have known to come back here to meet us! And, Chase! Look who's with him!"

"Lincoln and Toby," Chase said. "And Lori is with them! Milady? We are indeed safe!"

All four of them scrambled down the mountain, their energy renewed by the sight of the ship that would take them home.

And the reunion was joyous. Lincoln ran around the deck of the *Dawnwalker* in circles, until he flopped in exhaustion at Ari's feet. Captain Tredwell shook Ari's hand so long that she thought she'd get blisters. Toby greeted Chase and Rednal with three loud cheers. Lori danced around the deck and didn't ask once about getting back home to Glacier River. The celebration lasted until they were well under sail, headed toward the port of Sixton and home.

Toby, Ari, Chase, and Lincoln stood in the prow of the *Dawnwalker,* watching the waves slap the sides of the sturdy ship. Finn and Rednal stood a little way from them. The boy leaned comfortably against the unicorn's side, arms folded across his chest. Lori was talking happily to them both — but especially to Finn.

"Finn's gotten very fond of Rednal," Ari observed.

"And Lori of Finn!" Toby said in his usual blunt manner.

Ari laughed. "Finn's nice. And I know that

Chase and I wouldn't have been able to win the two challenges without him or Rednal. Will Rednal have to go back to the Celestial Valley, Toby?"

"All Celestial Valley unicorns have to go home eventually," Toby said. "We'll have to see what Atalanta says."

"You were telling me that the Watching Pool has been dark," Ari said anxiously. She held up the Scepter, which she hadn't let out of her sight. "Now that the Royal Scepter is back in Balinor, will the Watching Pool become clear again?"

"Maybe, maybe not," the carved wooden head said in a maddening way. "You are dealing with Deep Magic here, Your Royal Highness."

"Contrary little thing," Toby said in admiration. "What about it? Will the Dreamspeaker be able to watch in the pool again?"

"Yes," the Scepter said. "Her Royal Highness and His Majesty passed the trial by fire and the ordeal by moonlight, so, yes, the balance of magic has been restored."

"Does that mean that I will not be able to visit the Celestial Valley again?" Lincoln asked in a wistful way. He nudged his nose against Ari's side. "I wish you had been there, Ari. The Dreamspeaker was most gracious. I mean, she allowed Toby and me to return to Balinor to meet you here again, but she didn't say I couldn't return. The Celestial Valley is the most beautiful place you can imagine."

Ari faced into the wind. Her bronze hair trailed behind her. Chase was a reassuring presence at her back. "We *are* headed toward the most beautiful place, Linc. We are headed home to Balinor!"

About the Author

Mary Stanton loves adventure. She has lived in Japan, Hawaii, and all over the United States. She has held many different jobs, including singing in a nightclub, working for an advertising agency, and writing for a TV cartoon series. Mary lives on a farm in upstate New York with some of the horses who inspire her to write adventure stories like the UNICORNS OF BALINOR.